I0629111

SHOCK TREATMENT

Borgo Press Books by Ardath Mayhar

The Absolutely Perfect Horse: A Novel of East Texas (with Marylois Dunn)
The Body in the Swamp: A Washington Shipp Mystery [Wash Shipp #2]
Carrots and Miggle: A Novel of East Texas
The Clarrington Heritage: A Gothic Tale of Terror
Closely Knit in Scarlatt: A Novel of Suspense
Crazy Quilt: The Best Short Stories of Ardath Mayhar
Deadly Memoir: A Novel of Suspense
Death in the Square: A Washington Shipp Mystery [Wash Shipp #1]
The Door in the Hill: A Tale of the Turnipins
The Dropouts: A Tale of Growing Up in East Texas
The Exiles of Damaria: A Novel of Fantasy
Feud at Sweetwater Creek: A Novel of the Old West
The Fugitives: A Tale of Prehistoric Times
The Heirs of Three Oaks: A Novel of the Old West
High Mountain Winter: A Novel of the Old West
How the Gods Wove in Kyrannon: Tales of the Triple Moons
Hunters of the Plains: A Novel of Prehistoric America
Island in the Lake: A Novel of Native America
Khi to Freedom: A Science Fiction Novel
The Lintons of Skillet Bend: A Novel of East Texas
Lone Runner: A Novel of the Old West
Lords of the Triple Moons: A Science Fantasy Novel: Tales of the Triple Moons
Makra Choria: A Novel of High Fantasy
Medicine Dream: Being the Further Adventures of Burr Henderson
Messengers in White: A Science Fantasy Novel
Monkey Station: A Novel of the Future (Macaque Cycle #1; with Ron Fortier)
People of the Mesa: A Novel of Native America
A Planet Called Heaven: A Science Fiction Novel
Prescription for Danger: A Novel of the Old West
Reflections; & Journey to an Ending: Collected Poems
A Road of Stars: A Fantasy of Life, Death, Love, and Art
Runes of the Lyre: A Science Fantasy Novel
The Saga of Grittel Sundotha: A Science Fantasy Novel
The Seekers of Shar-Nuhn: Tales of the Triple Moons
Shock Treatment: An Account of Granary's War: A Science Fiction Novel
Slewfoot Sally and the Flying Mule: Tall Tales from Cotton County, Texas
Soul-Singer of Tyrnos: A Fantasy Novel
Strange Doin's in the Pine Hills: Stories of Fantasy and Mystery in East Texas
Strange View from a Skewed Orbit: An Oddball Memoir
Through a Stone Wall: Lessons from Thirty Years of Writing
Timber Pirates: A Novel of East Texas (with Marylois Dunn)
Towers of the Earth: A Novel of Native America
Trail of the Seahawks: A Novel of the Future (Macaque Cycle #2; with R. Fortier)
The Tulpa: A Novel of Fantasy
Two-Moons and the Black Tower: A Novel of Fantasy
Vendetta: A Novel of the Old West
Warlock's Gift: Tales of the Triple Moons
The World Ends in Hickory Hollow: A Novel of the Future
A World of Weirdities: Tales to Shiver By

SHOCK TREATMENT

AN ACCOUNT OF GRANARY'S WAR

A Science Fiction Novel

by

Ardath Mayhar

THE BORGO PRESS

An Imprint of Wildside Press LLC

MMIX

Copyright © 2009 by Ardath Mayhar

All rights reserved.
No part of this book may be reproduced in any form
without the expressed written consent
of the author and publisher.
Printed in the United States of America

www.wildsidepress.com

FIRST EDITION

CONTENTS

FOREWORD

The Romans used to tell their troops, "Be careful about killing a Celt—then you will have to deal with his wife." I suspect that one reason "civilized" countries have been reluctant to teach their women military skills is that when a woman fights you, she means to kill you. Or at the very least she means to civilize you.

—Ardath Mayhar
Chireno, Texas
April 2009

PROLOGUE

NOT AN EASY JOB

The trade representative stared down at the Commander of Station, as if reminding her that she was short and female and the leader of a world useful solely for its agricultural produce. "Madame Karmann, your document is...interesting." She could hear the sneer in his tone.

"It is also completely irrelevant. Your ancestors signed binding contracts with the United Worlds' Consortium of Traders, and those have not been and cannot be changed. Do not ask us to come down to this world again for further talk. This is a waste of time and energy not to be allowed. Our organization will not negotiate with you." He turned abruptly and motioned to his aide to follow him onto the pad where the shuttle waited.

Above, in geosynchronous orbit, was the platform to which the foodstuffs of Granary were regularly lifted by their single shuttle. There, in exchange, niggardly supplies of manufactured goods, raw metal, and medical supplies were deposited. Those grew skimpier every year, and Seleva Karmann felt certain that before long they would not be sufficient to sustain her farming population.

Food there was, in plenty, but tools and heavy equipment were necessary to continue producing it in quantities sufficient to sustain both the farmers and the space-faring fleets. Spacers depended upon unusual nutritional elements contained in the soil of Granary to maintain their health, even in the rapid transits now possible between worlds and systems. Experience had proved that concentrates and artificial nutrients could not supply needed elements.

Seleva suspected the great corporations profiting from the situation had forgotten that. Their captains almost certainly had. The arrogance of their representatives grew worse and worse. She knew she must do something, no matter what, to change the status quo. Ideas had appeared to her over the past several years, but they were not ones that an ethical person would consider.

Grinding her teeth, the diminutive Commander moved to the portal opening onto the launch pad. If she could have frozen it in place, trapped those thieving traders, forced them to negotiate in good faith...but that was a dream.

The shuttle was lifting from the single launch pad that served Station. Seleva watched its bulk lift awkwardly, battling gravity with its powerful engines. Her own people were trapped here, as much enslaved as those ancient peoples on their home world who had been bought and sold like cattle by the rich and powerful.

She sighed, feeling helpless. The position of Granary at the nexus of trade routes serving widely separated systems made it ideal for a supply station, and its uniquely fertile soil had made it vital for the trade. All it had lacked was a skilled force of farmers.

Now those who had been recruited for that work were little more than serfs, although their ancestors had been promised land, influential positions, and profits by their governments. The Commander and her family were confined there by the contract signed by her own grandparents. Her son and daughter were prisoners, as her grandchildren would be in time.

Turning from the portal, she slapped her hand on her desk, furious with the bare bones trade she had been forced to negotiate. According to that ancient contract, the Consortium of Traders set the terms, which were no more generous than they had been in the beginning. There was no provision in the document for renegotiation.

However, the population of Granary was growing. The original number of colonists had multiplied over a thousand years, and the farms were beginning to need more equipment, more training tapes, more medical training and supplies, more of everything that made for a civilized world.

A quizzical face peered around the corner of her study. "Angry again, eh, Seleva? Don't blame you. Don't blame you at all. Those fools are cutting their own throats. Put your mind to it and come up with a plan that will force them to rewrite the contracts. That's the only way you're going to get enough to keep us going."

She sighed. "Jeroboah, I have racked my brain, but I can't come up with any plan that will work. Not, at least, one that is honorable. Should I ignore my conscience in order to save my people?"

The elderly man wrinkled his forehead, making his age suddenly more apparent. "Remember, my friend, that sometimes responsibility must outweigh honor. That is not comfortable for a leader to contemplate, but ethical behavior must work in both directions. Think hard about this. You will, before the next shipment, find some method that will work for us, if I know you at all."

He frowned, his eyes suddenly very sharp and knowing. "The next ship's trading reps will know nothing of the decision this group made against having others of their sort come down on the shuttle. Remember that." Then he was gone.

She controlled her anger with some difficulty. That was the hardest lesson she was learning, since her election as Commander. There was work to do, and that would give her time to back away from her problems and look at them from a calmer perspective.

There was unrest in the Granges, which was increasingly common, for the workers were asked to do more and more and paid less and less. They had little enough on which to spend their scanty credits, she reflected. Even the food available for their families had been reduced, to meet the increasing demands of the Consortium.

This was their world, not the possession of the Consortium of Traders or United Worlds. There was no justice in the present situation, she decided, and with that she determined upon a rash and drastic move. If her honor was soiled, she thought, then so be it.

She must, however, wait for the next ship, with its representatives from the Consortium. This would be due in six months, in time for the major fruit harvest. Until then, she would deal with her Granges.

There were, she knew too well, elements among the farmers—even some Grangemasters who were in the pay of the Traders as spies and agents. Once she had her new contract, signed and irreversible, she must deal with such resistance. In order to do that, she feared she must harden her heart and do things that she would regret for the rest of her life.

* * * * * * *

Gadnor Keppel had been Grangemaster of Tellich for five years, and in that time he had found to his chagrin that it was nothing like as powerful a post as he felt his family deserved. His many times great-grandfather had been promised a fiefdom, when he signed the contract offered by United Worlds. Instead, he and his descendants found themselves grubbing in the dirt like peasants.

The Keppels were persistent people, bitter people, and over the generations their frustration had been handed down, as a family ritual, to all their children's children. Centuries had not dimmed the fire of their anger. When Gadnor received an offer from the Traders to work as their agent on Granary, with full assurance that he would receive a more than generous position and payment, he accepted it without hesitation.

He knew, of course, that Karmann intended to try renegotiating the ancient contract. If she had succeeded, he would have found a way to ingratiate himself with her, leading to some suitable result for himself. He was not disappointed when she failed, for the Traders offered much more than he could hope to wrest from the adamant Commander.

If the Commander pulled some devious action to undermine the Consortium's control over Granary's economy, he was in a position to organize resistance to her policies and to thwart her plans. There were others who were sick of laboring in the fields, grubbing for existence for little gain. He knew he could weld them into a force capable of taking over Station and controlling the flow of goods to and from their world.

Now, staring down at the planting schedules for the new crops of root vegetables, he smiled. Perhaps his opportunity would come soon, and he would find himself ousting that arrogant woman from Station and sitting in her office in the Citadel.

She was nearing middle age now. Her daughter was about to marry, and her son was not well, though he had a wife and a small boy. Gadnor was young, strong, vigorous; not she, nor any woman, was a match for him!

CHAPTER ONE

THE SILENT ROOM

He did not look like a madman. His thick-lensed glasses screened thoughtful silver eyes, and his face was unlined—too smooth for a man in his middle fifties. Yet something about his hands was vaguely frightening. The thick fingers gripped things too tightly, and the back-slanted thumbs, which earlier generations on another world had called the murderer's thumb, were disturbingly powerful.

As he studied the maps that moved on the console forming the tabletop, bending to squint at the constantly changing numbers and symbols that reflected engagements, casualties, supply lines, and troops, his hand beat time to music from a hidden speaker's antique music, played on ancient instruments. The melody was too delicate, one would have thought, for the taste of the Commander of Station.

Behind the console table/desk, the wall was filled with monitors, which revealed all the approaches to the complex that Standish called his Stronghold. Though he knew that other watchrooms were manned by people trained to note anything even remotely threatening, the Commander trusted nobody to be sufficiently alert. There were many who wanted his death, but he did not intend to die.

Theron Standish intended to survive, no matter what it took. He intended to unify forcibly the loose confederation of agricultural Granges forming this colony with the central force that was Station. His grandmother hated him for that, he knew. She had spent her life assuring the autonomy of each portion of this incredibly fertile world, after indulging in kidnapping and extortion in order to free Granary from the control of the Consortium of Traders.

Even as he thought it, he whirled and stared into a monitor to the left of the wall. Something was moving there, and his peripheral vision had caught the movement. Was it his grandmother, come again to torment him? He had exiled her to her home farm in order to keep from being forced to kill her.

Or was it that madman—that triple-damned Jeroboah—who had been the scholar appointed to oversee his education when Standish was young? The ancient philosopher/inventor appeared able to move as if invisible through the most intensely guarded and locked and electrified barriers, just as he had seemed to know at a distance when a younger Standish planned his cruel mischiefs. Theron felt one more encounter with him might shake his own reason.

But it was only Stefan Karmann, his cousin and second-in-command, coming with the nightly report, which was so secret that only one of the scrambled lines was secure enough to bring it into his hands. Only one tech was screened sufficiently to translate it. And no hand but Karmann's could be relied upon not to let it slip into other, less trustworthy fingers. Traitors were everywhere. Standish knew, and he could take no chance of betrayal.

Theron did not touch the button freeing his private door from its computerized lock until the shape of Karmann loomed in the monitor that covered the corridor outside. When the door hummed and the panels slid apart, the shape stepped forward...and was revealed to be, instead, a shrimp of a man, his face wizened with age, teeth yellowed where they were not missing entirely.

By what means had Jeroboah made himself seem to be another man? Standish felt his mind freeze for an instant with his old fear and hatred of his tutor. His body went stiff with shock. Though he was known as a scientist whose past achievements had given Granary the abilities it needed for defense, education, and efficient farming, the old man seemed, at times, more like a magician.

Jeroboah darted into the room, where Theron had shrunk back against his wall of monitors, and pivoted on unsteady legs to face the Commander. His tiny hand came out of his pocket, holding a shining tube. Another of his offbeat inventions? Fear chilled the Commander, as he looked into those bright, demented eyes.

Theron felt his heart bursting into his throat, his pulse thudding in his wrist. He would die! This time, he would die! Jeroboah had learned to deceive his electronic devices in the heart of the Stronghold, and it was the end!

The tube began to glow, a thin greenish light shining even through the hand holding it. Jeroboah grinned fiendishly at the Commander, as he twisted the knob at the end of the weapon.

The light turned scarlet. Theron braced himself for the end and Jeroboah said, "Bang!" Theron, waiting for death, tensed for it, almost wanting it now, felt something snap. His hand went up to touch another button, but before it reached its goal he fainted. Even as his senses dulled to black, he found himself wondering if this were reality or another indication that his mind was losing its balance.

* * * * * * *

Jeroboah's holographic image stood on the antique carpet, staring down at the jewel-toned flowers on which Standish lay. He moved to the Commander's side and wished this semblance of his could touch the Commander's elbow with a questing toe. But he was obviously still alive. That was good, for this was a game too amusing to end. Yet. He might be slightly mad, as he well knew, but he still loved a good joke.

He looked up at the monitors, where the ordinary life of the Stronghold went about its business. Between two of them hung a painting, which caught his eye with wistful recognition. A woman, beautiful and ancient, stared back at him as if she knew and approved what he had done. He had known her through her years of ruthless rule and her gradual reformation. They had been friends and allies for all her life.

Seleva. The Old One. Alive still? He didn't remember. But she had been a one, that woman. It was a wonder Standish had allowed her to live, after she abdicated her position in his favor. Or had he the ability to kill her at all? Others had tried and failed, many of them over the decades of her rule.

* * * * * * *

Standish stirred, and Jeroboah's image disappeared from the room. When Theron opened his eyes it was to find nothing amiss in his sanctum. The Commander pushed himself up with both hands, to stand beside the console. His glasses had fallen, and he fumbled blindly, bending to feel across the carpet until he located them. Then he stared about the room, up at the monitors, even at his grandmother's portrait, though he avoided meeting her bright silver eyes.

What had happened here? Was the stress of his great work affecting his mind? He shuddered and turned again to the lists, the movements, the many-faceted elements of his conquest of those who dared to prefer their own freedom to the achievement of his aims. If he was hallucinating, it was best kept to himself. And if he was not?

He refused to consider that possibility.

CHAPTER TWO

BLOODMUCK

The rumble and mutter of engines vibrated the air and the stony soil underfoot. The composite sole of Falville's boot conveyed the feeling into his toes, up through his legs into his belly. He groaned inaudibly and flopped into the roadside ditch.

The mud smelled of old deaths and too much blood. The tall weeds, nourished by the unexpected fertilizer of man flesh over the past months, made good cover, however, once he crawled out of the muck and into the higher side of the cleft. He slid backward, feeling on either side of him the movements of the men he led.

Beyond the shattered remnant of a fence there was a field of grain. Or had been. Most of it had been leveled by the firefight that had taken place there within the past few days. Falville had learned to gauge such things. No more than three days had gone by since the sizzling bolts and the pinging slugs had ripped through, harvesting the unripe grain.

Now the carriers were grinding up the slope, over the roads that had been well kept and smooth surfaced until the Commander had turned paranoid eyes toward the lush fields and the rich forests of Tellich Grange. What threat had he read there? Falville wondered, as he lay flat amid the shattered grain, hoping those now traveling over the pitted roads were not using heat-sensors as a precaution.

The sausage-shaped vehicles pounded forward on their tough treads, the one-way glass of their ports staring out over the countryside. Smoothly indented curves marked the spots where nozzles could open and flood the area about them with fire and death. For men armed only with weapons improvised from agricultural machinery and chemicals, it was impossible to stop.

About him, his men breathed so lightly that even he heard nothing but the chirp of a cricket in the hedgerow. The soil beneath his cheek quivered with the weight of the machines on the road. The leaves left on the grain shook, too, and the cricket went silent, as if even it might be threatened by the armored men who rode in the carriers.

He didn't risk an eye above the grain until the last had labored past, leaving its own contribution to the destruction of the roadway. In the distance, the metal tubes went forward over the low hill to the north, their camouflaged sides almost invisible against the dull greens of the fields and the forest.

Not even then did Falville signal his men to rise. He had learned painfully, over the months of the war, to distrust the enemy profoundly. What seemed to be, in dealing with the forces of Theron Standish, was never what was. Instead, he slithered around and headed toward the rear of the grain field, toward the low wall of trees marking the edge of Coldfellow Wood.

The Commander's men seemed to fear forests as much as their leader did. They avoided entering them, and they destroyed any forest in their way. But Coldfellow Wood was distant from the roads, far from any town or hamlet, and uninhabited except by those who lived by their wits in its depths.

Those had been people with prices on their heads, in days gone by, but now they might well turn out to be allies, for Standish hated and feared men who walked free in forests even more than the forests themselves. A day would come, and those shrewd mavericks knew it, when he would fire the trees from the Ellanish border to the Sterne Rift, just to destroy his combined devils.

They made good time through the wood. All too soon they left the sheltering trees in order to cut across fields and pastures to the encampment of the combined Resistance. Though Falville had urged his general to set up his command post deep in a forest, he had chosen instead to put it in plain sight, on a long stretch of stony pasture devoted to goats.

An earthen enclosure lay up against a cliff that formed the edge of a series of downs; it was sheltered there from the cold winds of winter and the glaring sun of summer. There General Coville put his headquarters, though the huts the goatherds had raised over the years were now little but accumulations of framework and brush.

Approaching the place, Falville had to admit it was an effective disguise for a military post. Goats ranged over the pasturelands, nibbling wild rosebushes to stubs, ignoring anything that came or went, and providing a good reason for the figures that moved, cloaked against the autumn chill, among the odoriferous groups of animals.

Their warm bodies misinformed any heat-sensing devices swept over the fields by occasional flying troops as well.

Anything less soldierly he could not imagine.

The guard lolled against a rock, a sling in his hand, his pose that of a watchful goatherd. He raised a hand, recognizing Falville, and nodded toward the General's hut. "Something's in the wind," he murmured as they went past, ducking beneath the level of the wall. "Coville's been wanting you for hours now. Best hurry, and don't take the time to eat or wash." He wrinkled his nose. "No matter that you need a good wash mightily. Been playing in the mud again?" His grin was sick, for he, too, knew the stench of the ditches of Tellich.

Falville gestured for his men to fall out and seek their own shelters. They would find food and wash water, if nothing else. For himself, he would have to wait. When the General called, he went, although until Standish invaded his country, he had been the least biddable of men.

General Coville stood firm, when all others had fallen or run. Now he alone, with his scattered groups of men and women, resisted the invaders. For that reason, Falville had given him his loyalty. To live in the world Standish intended to create here was not a thing he could imagine.

The hut was open to the air, its goatskin flap of door flung back and up onto the roof. Even with the chill of autumn beginning, the shelter of the down protected the spot. That kept the men from freezing, for they could not afford fires sufficient for all of them. Only a couple, suitable for those who ostensibly tended the goats, could be allowed, for too much smoke would inevitably bring a probing troop down upon them.

Inside, the dimness blinded him for a moment. Then the reddish glare of the tallow lamp picked out the faces around the rough table in the center of the room. There was Coville, huddled into his heavy coat, hands in his pockets, silent for once. There were Lemmon, the troopmistress, and Shoye, who trained and quartermastered the resistance, their enigmatic faces cautious and sharp lit with shadows. And there was Shemyona Fenn, the Chairwoman, last survivor of the ruling Grange of Tellich.

They were all staring at the woman who stood at the center of the group, gesturing. Her hand halted in midair, as Falville entered. He did not salute, for this was not a formal group worried about protocol. They worked together to save what they could of their crops and their people.

Nothing else mattered, and any notion one entertained that

might be helpful was welcomed by all, from Fenn to Coville.

"Seven carriers with fresh troops have moved toward the fort on Stormwall, each holding at least fifty men and their armor. A bitter blow that will be, when Stormwall falls, as it must. We have too few to resist for long."

Coville sighed and nodded. "You are right, Falville. But we have another matter to consider. This lady is the grandmother of Theron Standish. Seleva Karmann, mother of his mother, is here with a most surprising and useless proposal. And yet I find myself strangely tempted to do what she asks. See if you agree."

Falville turned to look at the woman, who had halted her speech as he came in. "Lady," he said. "What is it that you propose?"

She looked up a long way up, for she was very short and slight, into his eyes. Her own were a glint of silver between her eyelids, and her hair was also of that shade. Her face, however, was impenetrably, inevitably young, and the eyes shone with strength and purpose.

"I want to go into battle with you. I want to suffer with you, even die with you, if need be. I want to know with every cell in my body, every element of my mind and spirit just what happens when my grandson's machines and his men take a war to an innocent people in a country that was no threat to him or his. I am equipped with a device that will retain every sensation I encounter, and with it I hope to shock my grandson back to sanity."

The words jolted him. Deep inside himself, he felt that women had no place in battle, though more than half of those left to defend his country were female and were bearing arms at that moment. This fragile old creature surely could not endure what she proposed to do. Yet her eyes were filled with purpose. Suddenly he realized that she could and would, if he agreed with the others to allow her to go with them.

"Why?" he asked. The question rang in the room, as if it had been echoed in the minds of all those there.

"Because I want to know, to make my grandson know, what it is he is doing. I will not die, although my own body will serve as the accumulator for the electrical impulses of the dying. Not until the time is right. Our family has ways of surviving that most do not understand. I will gather the agony he sows across our world. Because of that, there is a chance, a very small, frail chance, that my grandson may be brought back to usefulness, in time, to undo what he can of the horrors he has caused.

"We will kill him if we must, but Granary will be the poorer. He is a brilliant man whose talents complement those I have used to make our world a free one. I broke the laws of honor and ethics, but I taught him how to keep from having to do that again. If he can be salvaged, we will all profit. Will you help me to see if this will work?" Falville stared down at her. The silver eyes gazed steadily into his.

This was the kin of the man he considered a monster. This woman had given birth to his mother, shared his blood. And yet...and yet he found himself persuaded, without more words, that she meant what she said. She intended to stop her grandson, in her own way, while he and his kind fought in their own.

"I will," he said, though he knew deep inside that no words spoken by any living being could divert the Commander from his purposes. The depth of his paranoia was obvious to all who had watched his actions.

A sigh of relief went around the room. The general grunted. "I am glad. We had agreed, already."

"Then we move toward Stormwall together. When?" Lemmon asked. She seemed to have taken on new definition with this immediate need for her services.

"As soon as we get our weapons and supplies together. Can you be ready?" the General asked Falville.

He sighed, thinking of his stinking clothing, his wet boots, his empty gut. Then he straightened his back. "We will go, whether we can or not," he said. "I'll tell my people. They needed to eat, but perhaps they have had time by now."

"And so do you," said the grandmother of the Commander. "You wash and eat. I will rally your troop."

Falville found himself provided with warm water, then pushed into a chair at the table and given a plate of goat meat and a tumbler of wine while the woman called his people. What a strange turn of events, he mused, as he drained the wine and stood again, just in time to hear the clink of weapons and the voices of those who were readying to go, once more, into battle.

The thought saddened him. His people were so ill-armed compared to the troops of the Commander. Only those living in Station had access to any of the weaponry available from the industrialized components of this vast cooperative of worlds. Granary was just what its name proclaimed, an agricultural world, supplied with little manufacturing capacity for civilian needs, for farming equipment, and for limited luxury items. Trading and military craft were supplied by many such worlds about the complex.

Station, the Commander's city, held the only port usable by the shuttle. That brought trade goods down from orbiting platforms, onto which the Traders deposited their goods and from which they picked up their loads of foodstuffs in payment. Until the Commander had begun to assume that every independent Grange on the continent threatened his position, the system had worked well for all. Now it spelled disaster for those who must rely on agricultural equipment factories to supply hastily devised weapons with which to confront the best the Cooperative of Worlds could provide.

And yet Falville did not hesitate as he finished his brief meal and rose to join his fellows. There was no question of surrender—they had seen what happened to Sterne Rift and to Ellanish, when their Granges tried to take that route.

Now the labor camps of those countries were filled with starving people, who worked until they died and were replaced with more captives. Surrender meant a slower and more demeaning death, and that was all.

He only hoped their deaths might mean something, when the terrible tale came to its end at last. Perhaps Seleva Karmann might do what the desperation of thousands could not, but how did she hope to persuade her mad grandson? Her suffering and that of others would mean nothing to him. The call came, and Falville went out to continue his war.

CHAPTER THREE

NEW USES FOR OLD BONES

Seleva trudged behind General Coville, protected on all sides by the ranks of men and women moving quietly westward through the wooded hills toward Stormwall. Her companions were without uniforms, without modern weapons, without anything but determination.

She ached for them...and for herself. Her legs were sturdy from a lifetime of walking and riding and, of late years, exercising in the gymnasium in her farmhouse. But her energies were not what they had been in her youth. The rough terrain was not like the rubbery smoothness of the flooring on which she had exercised.

She ached from neck to heels, though she would have died before admitting it to these tough, younger people who were going to their deaths on the escarpment holding Stormwall. Coville, ahead of her, had paused, and she came to a halt, hoping she could get her stiff joints moving again when the time came. She followed his gesture, as he pointed to a sharp ridge of rock rising beyond the treetops on their right.

"The scouts are there. They will let us know if Stormwall has fallen or is surrounded by the enemy. If that is true, we will approach through the trees," the general was saying to Falville and Lemmon. "That will provide cover until we are across the valley and near the cliff. Then we can run like mad and hope we're not cut down before we get under the precipice. They'll be watching, but perhaps they won't expect us so soon. They didn't see you, I assume."

Falville shook his head.

"Then this is the best we can do. Shoye!"

The stocky quartermaster appeared at his elbow. His eyebrow

was quirked irritably as he came to a halt.

"Everyone has rations for two days? And ammunition for the pellet guns?"

Shoye looked disgusted. "What do you think my job is, General? Tattooing roses on my butt? Of course. They're as ready as I can get them, considering what we have to work with."

Falville touched the General's sleeve. "The new grenade launchers should help, Sir. We tried those out, down in the old quarry, and they worked tremendously well. They don't leave a trace as they go in, and they really tear things up when they hit. I think that is going to be a development the Commander's people aren't expecting and won't know how to cope with. At least for a while." He thought of the rugged stone walls of the fortress atop the narrow ridge of cliff and sighed.

"I have the bowmen already briefed. They're moving ahead of us right now, and they'll take up their positions on the high ground. That should give them the ability to see the area around the fortress. They'll stay put and give the enemy something to think about while the rest of us dash across the valley to get under the overhang."

Seleva sighed and wiped her face on her sleeve. She had seen those heavy compound bows and the grenades the fertilizer factories had managed to create from agricultural chemicals. They were deadly, but they had to be lit inside the cups of tinder before being launched. She hoped none of the bowmen and women would join their victims in the rain of blood and body fragments that was sure to follow the attack.

Coville nodded and gestured his immediate group forward. She sighed again as she picked up one heavy and reluctant foot and placed it in front of its fellow. Blast and damn her grandson!

* * * * * * *

They arrived at the hem of the wood in late afternoon, slipping by ones and twos into the best cover they could find. Coville insisted that she remain behind the stony outcrop halfway up the ridge, as much for the convenience of his troops as for her own protection. She would, she knew, be a liability in battle. But the device she had stolen from Jeroboah would work from that distance, she was sure. Its range was, the inventor had assured her, good up to two miles, unless mountains intervened.

The silver box hooked to her belt was an insane thing, which could only have been conceived by a demented mind. Jeroboah called it the Neuroresonant Accumulator, and he had explained it as a receiver for the powerful brainwaves generated by human pain. The body of the wearer served as a focus, transferring the intensified energy into the receptors inside the box. Every time one of these people died, she would feel every aspect of that death, her old body struggling to maintain itself against the agony. She would not die, in truth, but she must suffer death repeatedly.

The higher ground was now strung with a thin line of hidden archers. From slightly below them, she watched as the dark-clad people waited for dusk, which might help hide their movements. She could see motion on top of the precipice that formed Stormwall. The escarpment cut diagonally across the western reach of the continent, between the mountains and the sea, topped by the old fortress walls erected by the earliest colonists against possible enemies, who did not, in truth, exist at all.

There was armor there, moving along the road that crossed its top. Turrets and nozzles were visible from time to time as the tracked vehicles followed the crooked way. She had been there, long before, and recalled the places where jutting stone outcrops thrust up, making the path bend drunkenly. The long cylinders of the carriers would be hard to work around them.

Those things up there possessed laser beam generators and armaments she had only read about in the catalogs the Consortium sent to its member worlds. Nasty things like disruptors that would tear the hopeful farmers manning the fortress to shreds or burn them to cinders.

And these people whom she had come to know would be destroyed, too, if those weapons were brought to bear upon them too soon. She found herself praying to the obsolete gods of her ancestors and clenched her teeth. She knew, as did most in her day, that you must will your own destiny, if it is to be achieved. The problem with that belief was, of course, that a madman could divert and distort many destinies other than his own.

The sun was halfway behind the rough hillocks to seaward, now, and its red glow was diffused by high cloud. It was almost time....

* * * * * * *

The cloud thickened, and darkness dropped like a blanket, as a mist drove in from the sea on the evening breeze. It was the best of luck for the attackers, and Seleva felt the stirrings of many bodies, as they tensed to obey the signal that would send them dashing across the barren strip dividing the tree line from the rocky space at the foot of the declivity.

A faint birdcall shrilled, almost deadened by the fog. There was the simultaneous twanging of bows, the rush of thick arrow shafts, and the fort's walls bloomed into scarlet explosions. Seleva could see a carrier explode, burning as it plunged off the edge to bounce down the rough cliff and hit with a roar as it struck the rubble below. Arriving explosive had evidently met liquid fuel.

She could not see the troops as they rushed across the red-lit fog in the valley, but she knew they were on their way. She had not suspected the depth of anger and despair that her grandson had aroused in their normally peaceful people, and now the numbers willing to die to keep their freedom astonished and appalled her.

She settled back into the hollow behind the outcrop and thumbed the control of her device. Jeroboah did not know she had stolen it. His growing mental disability meant that he could recall little that had happened in the past and not much of his own present. She doubted he remembered their friendship. Yet this invention might mean the saving of many lives. She closed her eyes and let the electronic receptor field control her mind and her nerves.

The immediate sensation was fear turning, almost immediately, to pain as distant minds reacted to the terrible things done to their bodies. She gasped, as the mind she had touched boiled away in a stream of flame from above.

She hated feeling others dying! She hated suffering! But that seemed to be the task set for her, here at the end of her days. Again and again and again!

CHAPTER FOUR

A DARKNESS FILLED WITH DEATH

Falville felt his ankle turn as his boot slid sideways on a stone. He gave a heave and crashed heavily against a groin of rock, safe beneath the slight outward bulge of the cliff. He heard, around him, panting breaths, crunching stones, and the impact of other bodies against unyielding rock.

The echoing blasts from the top of the cliff continued, as more grenades were lofted against the road around the fortress. Now there was also fire directed downward toward those sheltering against the stone, and the stink of the oily fuel of the manburner was sickening. The flaming carrier, from which cries and moans no longer came, gave enough illumination for the enemy above to aim their streams of energy and their bolts of fire at their attackers below.

A streak of brightness licked down the cliff side, and the dark shape to his right shrieked. He could hear the sizzle of the body fat, as the beam burned the woman to a shrunken wisp. He wanted to vomit, but he had no time. His people must move now, or they would die here uselessly.

He aimed upward, pointing his improvised catapult weapon at a groin of rock high above his position. The thing gave a quiet cough, and a projectile whizzed high, towing a length of cable. He was lucky, for it blew itself a hold into the stone of the cliff, and when he tugged hard the connection held.

Around him, other launchers fired, and more cables snaked upward, then down from their anchorages. Falville whistled, the sound cutting through the din of falling rock and groaning wounded and roaring energy beams from above. Without waiting, he began to go up the sheer wall, trusting his weight and his life to the line and the grapnel. Others, too, were on their way up. He heard their grunting breaths and the occasional curses, as well as the grating of boots as they scraped against the rock.

For some strange reason, he found himself thinking of the Commander's grandmother as he struggled up the cliff. It was no time for such lollygagging, he knew, but he had the strangest feeling that she was looking over his shoulder.... Something clattered toward him, directly overhead, and he twisted sideways on his cable, trying to avoid it. A stone bounced off his shoulder and on down the cliff, leaving his arm half numbed, as he swung back against the wall and hung on, trying to get some strength back into his grip.

He heard someone else fall. There was no outcry as the body plunged past, and he wrenched his thought away. If he and his people were to live or at least to die to some effect, they had to get up this wall of rock and into the rubble that topped the cliff.

He flexed his arm. Still numb. He pulled himself up with his left hand and reached the spot where the grapnel had anchored itself. Once there, he stared up into the smoky darkness, where the outlines of the stones above him appeared in reddish outline. It looked passable.

He whistled shrilly, the sound cutting through the roar and hiss of the beams from above. All of his people still able to move would be struggling up toward him.

The hand moved at last, not well but enough to steady him as he gripped with the other one. He climbed farther up, dug in his heels, climbed again. There was still a slight bulge above him, and he knew he must circumnavigate it, but for now it deflected the flame licking down toward his position. The rounding of that bulge was something he refused to think about. If he fell, then he must die, and that was that.

He felt with cautious hands and feet, edging around, finding purchase, edging again. Behind him, he could hear labored breathing that told him someone else was close on his heels. Then he was staring upward at the point from which the beam was issuing, now off to his right. There was a crevice alongside, into which he worked his way and continued upward, as if climbing a chimney.

It ended in a ledge formed by a boulder spanning its width. He stood up cautiously, to find his head almost at the top of the rock; only a slight upward heave brought his eyes level with a point at which he could see about him. There were still carriers moving along, their shields locked into place behind the ports, blinding those inside, except for the road directly ahead. Groups of armored men, their thermal shielding bulky in the chaotic light, huddled around the two beamers that were backed to the cliff edge a hundred yards apart, so as to focus their fire downward.

No one was looking to the sides, as far as he could see. Anyone who did would be blinded by the fires of their neighbors' weapons. Staring into the darkness would show them nothing.

Taking the chance, he heaved himself upward onto the surface of the cliff. Behind him there was another grunt, and he rolled out of the way of Gillen, who was a goatherd when she was not being a warrior.

"Where?" she whispered.

He pointed toward the road, where the last of the carriers had now passed. The dim lights were receding toward the fortress, which was now enveloped in smoke and flame from the grenade launchers. So great was the tumult ahead that he felt sure no one in the carriers would spare any thought for anything behind.

"Watch. Then cross," he said. "Wait for reinforcements. We'll come up the other side of the road, behind the troops who are attacking those below us. Push them off the edge...." but she was gone already, eeling over the rough terrain to disappear into the darkness.

When no more came up the chimney or could be heard below, Falville turned to follow those who had crossed already. There were fifteen of them, waiting there with Gillen for further orders. He hunkered low behind a sheltering boulder and gestured for them to bend close.

"Work down the line. Half of you form behind this nearest group of armor, half behind the other. They know we are few, and they won't spare more than they have to for this small an operation. They're going to concentrate on getting inside the fortress before the rest of us can reach it to reinforce the people there. When you hear the whistle, rush them. Don't waste slugs; push all of them over, if you can manage it. And then follow me toward the fortress. We'll surprise them, if we can."

They said nothing, but half the group melted into the night, and only the noise of the beams and the crackling of seared rock reached his ears. He counted steadily—forty-five, forty-six, forty-seven, forty-eight, forty-nine, fifty!

He whistled again, the carrying signal used by the foresters and herdsmen among whom he had grown up. He rose, crouched into a protective huddle, and dashed toward the wide backs bending over the controls and the nozzle of the weapon. He surged into the nearest, knocking the unsuspecting tech off his feet. The edge of the precipice was only a yard away, and the desperate man, realizing his danger, twisted frantically backward, trying to find a handhold before he pitched over it.

On either side, others were struggling with their attackers, trying to reach hand weapons they had not thought to need at their present task. Falville dropped to his knees and shoved the bulky body with all his might, sending it over into space. A long cry rose, ending in a soggy crunch, and Falville turned to help his people.

Only five techs had manned this weapon, and his seven people had overcome them all. Three had gone to join their fellow below and the fourth, who wore the flash of a weapons master on the overtunic concealing his body armor, was captured. This would be a valuable prisoner, if they could secure him long enough to have him interrogated by Shoye. The drugs that experimenters had derived from native weeds of Granary had proven useful for many purposes, not the least of which was the loosening of tongues.

The beam weapons were still bellowing their fires into the darkness below. Falville was not familiar with the devices, but he felt about, trying to find a switch that would stop the outflow of fuel. The valve was there, and soon the licking flame dwindled. Set properly and made usable, this thing could cut off those who manned the carriers ahead from any support coming up behind.

Gillen, perceptive as always, set her shoulder beside his, and they were joined by the others as they heaved the bulky thing around to aim its deadly nozzle across the road.

"How do you ignite the thing?" asked Fleck, who seemed able to conquer almost anything mechanical. His fingers were already moving over the control panel, feeling out the various settings and avoiding the valve that adjusted the flow of fuel. Before Falville could reply, he gave a small grunt and a chuckle.

"Never mind. I found it. It's no problem at all—an idiot could use the thing."

"Which is why Standish's fools can use it." Falville turned to face the man. "You stay here, Fleck. We'll need you to keep anyone from coming up behind us. Do you need any help with the nozzle?"

"Not set the way it is. They were playing it down the cliff, and that took manpower. I can shoot it right across the road, and if I need to angle it toward oncoming traffic, I can shove the whole thing around a bit. No problem, Sir. Can do."

It was a great comfort to have his line of retreat secured. Any new arrivals on the scene would be signaled by the firing of the flamer, which would give ample warning of trouble to come. And then what? He shrugged and ran forward.

The rest of his attack group was waiting in a semicircle of boulders between the north wall of the fortress and the drop. The space was too narrow and rough for any vehicle and provided no route for anyone on foot to escape toward the east, so the men from the carriers had left it unguarded. It was perfect as a staging point for their own activities.

The looming wall of the installation screened the end of the curve of stones, allowing Falville to find a concealed position from which to signal those inside the fortress. This time he used a modified skyrocket for his purpose, sending the sputtering thing, dug from his pack, over the wall at a low angle, so as to be invisible to those beyond the barrier.

After some time, a line dropped down the wall, with a message cylinder attached. Falville sent his information aloft with that and turned again to his small troop. The carriers had positioned themselves, once their contents were unloaded, in order to blast the westward wall of the fortress with laser beams from their turret weapons. It would take little of that sort of fire to penetrate the stone, which was already crackling and popping as internal moisture expanded and seams were driven apart by the pressure.

* * * * * * *

Seleva lay gasping in her nook on the hillside, trying to get her breath. The action of the past hours had been so intense that she felt as if she had been sucked along by a tornado, whirling madly in its destructive tail.

The night was waning now, and Falville and his people were waiting for a signal from the fort before attacking the Commander's men on the road. That gave her a chance to rest a bit, assuring her quivering flesh it had not suffered personally any of the devastating injuries she had been experiencing through the device. She knew, now, how it felt to be seared to ash by a beam weapon. She had died three times, each death different in detail but similar in outraged astonishment before peace followed it. She found it impossible to stand up, for her body had accepted itself as terribly wounded. It was impossible to make it return to normal simply by willing it.

She had not realized, before this day, how much of what the body experiences is simply the perception of the mind. Actuality, she began to suspect, might be a far different thing from what the senses and the brain conceived it to be. This was the sort of thing that the philosopher she had once been could appreciate, but the warrior she was again becoming could not spare the time to pursue it. She must sleep, or the next spurt of action might well kill her, through stress.

She was, after all, very old, no matter how fine her health might be. And she must live to take this device, with its trapped agonies, to her grandson.

CHAPTER FIVE

REPORTS

The stronghold had been reinforced with more guards, better electronic sensors, more monitors. Standish was certain no one could reach him in his private complex now. That madman Jeroboah would be frustrated in his insane attempts to frighten the ruler of Station. The new precautions he had installed would thwart anyone.

A sonata was trilling its notes—Telemann, this time. Standish had a penchant for the more mathematical of the ancient composers. He nodded in time to the music, as he studied the readout from the most recent engagement.

Stormwall was all but in his hands, of course, no matter how desperately the peasants defended it. Now that his troops were in place, it could not matter how many others came from the countryside to climb its walls and throw their puny bodies against his forces. They could not defeat modern weaponry. This was merely a delay, a very slight one, he was sure, before the end of resistance in Tellich.

There came a chirp from an adjacent monitor, and he touched a key, activating the screen. Karmann's square face sprang into focus. There were lines about his eyes, bracketing his mouth, that had not been there yesterday.

Theron Standish frowned. "Yes?" His tone was harsh. Not even with his cousin did he allow any hint of humanity to show through his veneer of frozen calm.

"The troops up on Stormwall are trapped. Reinforcements are being destroyed by a beam weapon—it has to be one of ours. Groups of the rebels have dug in up and down the top of the escarpment to harry our armor. They have captured at least three carriers with their weapons systems intact.

"Stormwall is, for all practical purposes, delivered from our siege and unrecoverable at this time." Karmann did not look happy. He stared from the screen at Standish. "Our grandmother is not to be found. She left her home in the Vineyard two days ago, and no servant has told us where she went. We have only one of them left alive, and I have decided that since neither the drug nor torture has loosed their tongues, they truly did not know."

Standish slapped his hand flat on the desktop. "I haven't enough problems with this rebellious world to tame and these ignorant peasants to put in their places—no, I must also be deviled by a crazy grandmother, who should have been put in restraints long ago!

"Find her, Karmann, and lock her away in her own house, with our own people to make certain she does not escape. If our enemies should get their hands on her, they might think they had some leverage over me. It might make them bold."

He paused for a long moment. "Kill her if you must."

Karmann looked even more unhappy, but he nodded. "I will do my best," he said. "But you know Seleva. She might be anywhere, doing anything. She is not your usual old woman, content to sit by her fire and play with her cat. You are younger than I. You do not remember her as she was."

Standish grunted. He remembered her too well, even though he had been a child when she negotiated that altered agreement with the Traders, when she became Commander. One of the things that had shaped his character was the way she got the terms she wanted from the Traders' Consortium by kidnapping their team of negotiators when they came down to parlay with her.

He almost chuckled. She held them hostage until their companies allowed the most favorable terms ever granted a food-producing world. Autonomy was not something they had ever before granted to such a planet. Trace minerals in Granary's soils proved to be necessary for human health in space. Only that fact and her ruthlessness allowed that loose confederation of Granges to grow strong enough to do the things he was now attempting.

Other agricultural worlds whimpered about the heels of the Consortium of Traders, begging the Consortium for relief from their dismal economies when the Traders grew stingy with trade goods. His was the single one that could cooperate with the others or go it alone, without fear of reprisal.

The contract she forced from the Traders was ironclad, and to breach it would be to destroy the very foundation of the Consortium. She had studied the laws governing the Traders, and closed every hidden loophole the contracts contained. They wept, but they signed, for she would have hanged every one of those hostages if they had not. He did not underestimate his grandmother. It frightened him that she should be missing.

Standish clicked down a key and Karmann's face was gone. The man was dependable, it was true. He had a dog-like affection for his younger cousin. But he was a worrier...that was his worst weakness. If he continued to allow the vagaries of an old woman to distract him from his duties, he would become expendable. Sad.

Theron sighed and returned to the casualty lists, the tallies of lost equipment. The tale the readouts told was not favorable, and he began to drum his fingers on the polished wood, in time to the music. Something would have to be done, not only about those stubborn holdouts on Stormwall, but also about his no less rebellious ancestress. She had been a thorn in his side for long enough.

It was time sheer old age took her to her grave. Who would care, or would dare to say a word if he did care, if one single, gray-haired female ceased to breathe? He tapped a code into one of the keyboards, and a screen lit up, without showing the face behind it.

"Cozarre, I have a task for you."

There came an anonymous grunt from the machine.

"You know my grandmother, Seleva Karmann? I want her to...reach her peace at last. She has gone missing, but I am certain you can find her if you take your Sniffer and put your mind to it. When you do, make certain she gives me no more problems. Ever." Theron smiled gently and again nodded to the rhythm of Telemann's sonata.

There came another grunt from the communications system, assuring him that his order had been heard and understood. Cozarre had never failed him, and he had no doubt that this order, too, would be successfully carried out. More than one unmarked grave was filled with the assassin's victims, removed from Standish's path by his trusted killer.

As to Stormwall, the Commander of Station had more than one sort of weaponry at his command. Those who flew the machines the Traders had brought in their last shipment, before becoming so cautious with their more sophisticated equipment, were about to come into their own.

* * * * * * *

In his ramshackle house, which not a single member of Standish's staff or guard had ever inspected, so obviously derelict it seemed, Jeroboah leaned back comfortably in a tattered chair. He watched the many tiny monitors that pocked the walls surrounding him. One, set at a convenient angle, covered all of Standish's Stronghold from drill-ground to the inner sanctum of the Commander.

The gnomish man chuckled. How distraught the Commander would be if he knew that his archenemy had tapped into the frequencies of every element of the surveillance equipment. Not only could he observe his prey without effort, he could also mislead and monitor any of those guardian mechanisms, using only his pocket-sized computer. He had, after all, invented the systems used to construct it.

The memory of Standish's look when he saw, instead of his cousin, his worst tormentor standing at his door was one that Jeroboah treasured, even though he had been present only as a hologram and had viewed it through Standish's own monitoring system.

Today was one of the good days, the inventor decided. He remembered clearly a number of things that tended to become lost in the tangle of his mind. He knew, for instance, that Seleva Karmann was, indeed, alive. He suspected she had been the one who took his least orthodox invention from its cabinet and carried it away, on her last visit to him. How like her: only Seleva would use her own body in order to activate it. He had a suspicion concerning the use to which she might put it, and that thought filled him with boyish glee.

Being erratic was sometimes a problem, he had found, but there was nothing like it for keeping one's life interesting. He might forget to eat. He might lose his friends through the crannies of his ancient mind, but he would never lose sight of his main purpose in life, which was making life miserable for Theron Standish.

* * * * * * *

Falville lay on a cot, holding himself still by a gargantuan effort. The burns that had seared his entire left side, as molten rock poured over him, had left the damaged nerves screaming, though he had managed, so far, to keep his jaws locked over his cries. The remnants of his people lay about the walls, few unwounded, all weary and yet smiling.

The siege was broken. Stormwall was free of the Commander's troops. Scorched hulks of several carriers, still filled with smoking carcasses of the men inside, littered the space about the walls, which were damaged badly, and many of the defenders were damaged almost as severely.

The physician who had attended those assigned to the fortress was dead, killed in one of the sweeps of liquid flame the carriers had cast. The other, who had come with the general's people, was exhausted. He had tended burns and wounds from bursting rock fragments and shock and head injuries from falls until he had dropped where he stood. Seleva looked exhausted, eyes heavy with fatigue. It seemed to Falville that she felt, inside herself, the agonies he had endured, as well as those of his fellows on the row of cots running down the dim-lit corridor. Her face was paper pale, lined deeply, her eyes purple-shadowed. From time to time she quivered, very slightly.

If Falville had not been concentrating on her, trying to take his mind totally away from his tortured body, he would not have noticed those movements. As it was, he became so fascinated by her reactions, timed precisely to the worst twinges from his burns, that he began to intuit what it was that she had done.

He gestured for her to bend over him, and she came to his side at once. "What do you need?" she asked.

"How is it...that you feel...what I feel?" he gasped. "You do. I have...seen it. How?"

She frowned, and his own surge of pain was reflected in her silver eyes, as she braced herself against the flood of agony. When the worst had passed, she straightened, and her hand went to an ornament hooked to her belt. She detached a small box from the thing and held it for him to see.

"This is an unusual device," she said. "It gathers suffering into a focus, using me as its lens. It stores that pain against a future need, when it can be transferred to another nervous system."

"But why should you need such a thing?" Falville asked, staring at the shining thing. "What use is it?"

"There will come a time when I will have need, believe me," she said. "Now here is your medication. It is time at last to ease your pain."

She lifted his head, and he burned and shrieked internally and drank. Darkness was welcome, when it came.

CHAPTER SIX

STORMWALL

Seleva had read the situation at Stormwall accurately, even before General Coville called a meeting of his officers. She was included as a matter of courtesy, even though her project was obscure and personal and highly questionable. When she went into the central chamber where the walls still stood, unpenetrated by the searing beams of the energy weapons, she found a much diminished group gathered about the table that Coville was using as a desk.

He looked up as she entered, and she could see he was both exhausted and worried. "You have had news," she said, before he could speak. "And it has not made you happy."

He widened his lips, but it was not a grin. "You might say that," he agreed. "My people in Station have sent word that the Commander is readying his flying troop. We cannot withstand an attack from the air, Mistress Karmann. That is obvious. The walls would have been breached entirely if the ground attack had lasted an hour longer."

"So you must withdraw your people at once, in order to keep from losing any more," she said. Her tone was sharp and commanding, and he seemed surprised at her insistence. "To lose Stormwall will open the northern reaches, the entire grain-growing area, to the inroads of the Commander. The only way to stop him is to starve him out. Station is limited in its capacities for crops. Foodstuff has always been brought in for the local inhabitants. With the grain fields in his hands, the Commander will be much harder to bring to a halt.

"My grandson is a hard man to stop anyway," she said. "Believe me, I have tried since he was a child to stop his more outrageous errors of behavior. But losing the people here on Stormwall is simply going to weaken you, without keeping the grain farms out of his grasp. If you withdraw your people into Coldfellow Wood, avoiding the roads and the open fields, his flying troops cannot locate you easily from the air." Her tone held the assurance of her long years of management on this specialized world.

The General stared at her, turning pale. She hastened to reassure him as much as possible. "I understand that their sophisticated surveillance equipment never was brought on planet. The Traders claimed they were in short supply, but it might be that someone in the Consortium suspects that Theron has gone mad. I would withhold such weaponry and equipment from anyone who might pose a problem for me, believe me."

Coville looked down at the maps on the table. "I have been considering it," he said. "If I leave a small group here to resist as long as possible...."

"They will be killed and lost to your cause," Seleva said. "Run, General. Run like mad, taking all your people with you, the wounded too. I do not trust my grandson to deal gently even with those no longer able to fight against him. Take them beyond his reach or kill them. Either is better than the things Standish is capable of inventing for them."

His bushy brows rose. "You truly believe he would abuse my wounded?"

"I know he would," she said. "Get ready, and go as soon as you can. I have a bad feeling about this. Things are moving against us, even now. My advice, though I have no right to offer it, is to get into the wood."

Lemmon spoke from the shadows. "I agree, General. And Shoye and I have devised a way to carry the wounded in fair comfort. Wet, oiled sheepskins rolled about them should keep those who are badly burned from the worst of their pain. We have enough air litters to carry them all. If we're alive, we can keep fighting. If we're dead, we're out of it, and there's nothing more we can do."

Shoye nodded agreement, his eyes dark-shadowed but alert.

"Then we will go. It is what I wanted to do, but I hesitate even now to leave the fortress." The general sounded weary.

"Then blow it." That voice came from the doorway, and it was shockingly familiar.

"Falville! How did you get here? You couldn't move without screaming." The General rose and put a steadying hand beneath his elbow; the officer winced at the pressure.

"False skin. There is a bit of it left, and Seleva here made them use some of it on me. She claimed I was needed. I'm not much good, but I can walk and talk, and maybe I can oversee blowing up the fortress. It is almost wrecked, as it is."

Shoye grinned savagely, teeth glinting in the light. "We will go together," he said. "And I will set the charges where you advise me to. If we have the time, we will bring it down. If we do not, we will bring it down on top of us."

Coville stared at the pair for a moment. Then he nodded. "Get busy. I'll start everything else."

Seleva smiled and turned back toward the hall where the wounded were kept. It was going to be tough, moving them over rough terrain. Burns were so painful—she would gather a lot of fresh agony for her device, as she helped to get these wounded into cover.

But she stopped at the door, overtaken by a sudden inspiration. She turned to stare at Coville. "Have you succeeded in making contact with the rebels in Coldfellow Wood?" she asked him.

His face turned even grayer, and the lines about his eyes deepened. "No. I have sent several emissaries, and only one returned. He was still alive...just enough to pass on the word to me. And then he died. They do not take kindly to anyone, those refugees in the wood. They have not been kindly treated by the Granges."

"Then allow me to go to them. If they kill me, I am only one old woman, no loss to your troop strength. If they do not, simply because I can pose no threat to them, perhaps I can persuade them their best chance for survival lies with us, rather than alone against Theron's resources."

Falville made a sudden gesture, cut off quickly because of the pain it caused him. Coville bent his head and stared down at the map before him. Neither spoke for a moment.

Lemmon came to stand beside Seleva. "I am not dangerous to look at. I could go with Madame Karmann to Coldfellow Wood. Together, it may be that we can make those stubborn people realize it is not only they who stand at risk now. The whole world will go, in time, if Standish is victorious.

"He has not the judgment to consolidate his conquered peoples and make them work together productively. He will enslave everyone, destroy too much, work to death all those who do not rebel and die fighting him. Let me go, General. We will have a better chance of returning, I think, than any men you might send to try to insure safe passage through the forest."

Coville looked up from the map. His big brown hand spanned the space between the fortress and the high country beyond Coldfellow. "This is the only route. Any other would take us across cleared fields or along roads, and that would invite disaster. I would never allow this, if I thought there were any other way. Now I say 'yes.' Both of you may go, but only after you take the time to reconsider. You may never return, believe me."

Seleva nodded, her face grim. "I believe you, General Coville, I know those rebels better than you. Some used to be workers on my family's farms, before Theron grew so great. They have good reason to hate and fear him. They have no reason to hate me, for they know that I tried all I could to stand between them and my mad grandson."

Lemmon pushed past her into the corridor. With a weary shrug, the old woman followed her, as the troopmistress hurried to delegate her own duties among her troops. "I will find packs and a few supplies for us, in case we are cut off before we gain our goal," Seleva said to her retreating back. "I will meet you by the offal gate on the lowest level of the fortress, when I am ready. It will be dark soon, and we should be able to leave without being seen, even if Theron has set spies to watch."

* * * * * * *

It was entirely dark when she heard Lemmon's boots grating against the stone of the floor. On this lowest level, where prisoners were kept and sometimes tortured in the days before the old colony came fully under the more civilized control of the Consortium, the only light came from her hand-generated electric torch. As she squeezed the handle of the generator, she saw Lemmon's square face blossom against the dark.

"All ready," grunted the troopmistress. "Where's your gate?"

Seleva moved to the seemingly blank wall at the end of the low corridor and reached upward. A chain met her fingers, and she hooked into it and pulled downward. The counterweight almost swung her off her feet, and the younger woman came to lend her weight, as a square doorway was revealed by the sliding panels that closed it from the outer air.

From this hidden slot, the bodies of the dead, the garbage from the kitchens farther down the corridor, and various spies had been ejected from the fortress over the generations of its use. As they went through the opening, stooping almost double, Seleva recalled the featureless wall that showed from inside and out by day. Clever people, the ancestors of her kind, she thought.

Then they were out in the cold air of Stormwall, standing in a sheltered pocket behind the dense walls and hearing the wind whistle past the crenelations high above them. Off to the south and east, the hills bulked along the skyline in a black wall that patterned itself against the stars.

"We will go along the old track the outlaws used to take to cross Stormwall," said Seleva, almost to herself. "If it is still there...."

"It is," said Lemmon. Her firm hand shot out of the night and took Seleva's arm. "Let me hold onto you. Neither of us wants to be lost from the other. We can't go calling aloud. Come this way. I suspect I have traveled that route since you have."

Seleva grimaced. "Some half century since, in fact," she said. "Come, my child, let us move. We must clear the road for our people, and we have so little time."

The ornament at her waist gave a sudden throb of agony, which acted as a stimulant to her faltering body. Straightening, Seleva Karmann moved beside the troopmistress into the precipitous track leading down from Stormwall. The wind picked up strength out of the north and pelted them with dead leaves and grit blown from the top of the escarpment.

CHAPTER SEVEN

COLDFELLOW WOOD

Arvid Strindberg sat in the top of a tree, staring off toward the distant bulk of Stormwall. Something had been going on there—flares of energy had lighted the night sky, fires burned in places where no flames should be, and the sound of shattering rocks had crackled even into the reaches of the surrounding forest. The disturbance had been so long-lasting and furious that the lookouts in this northernmost part of the wood had sent for their leader. Something was in the wind, and it boded no good for those who sheltered among the trees.

The war in the fields and pastures, the hills and valleys of Tellich, had not yet extended into their domain, but Strindberg knew the time would come when it must. The rumors gathered by those he sent into marketplaces and farming communities had been filled with desperate foreboding, though with little hard information.

Though it had not been recently when the last such informant had found his way back into the wood, Strindberg had put together all the things he had heard. He assembled all the facts he knew about those involved in the areas surrounding Station and his personal knowledge of the reality that was Theron Standish. Now he felt he knew what was happening, to some extent.

It did not make him happy to know his suspicions were probably correct. But that prolonged combat on Stormwall told him much. The people of Tellich were resisting Standish. What it was that Standish proposed to do with conquered areas of Granary eluded his logical processes, but Strindberg had a gut feeling it was nothing good, either for the people or the planet. He had learned long since that Standish was a megalomaniac.

It had been his mother who precipitated the disaster, strangely enough. She was a healer and herbalist, known throughout the truck farming area for her success with fevers and suppurating wounds. She was also beautiful in the way that some women grow into, as they age with grace and wisdom and self control.

Standish had been brought to her with a broken collarbone, after falling from an inspection platform at the local fair, some ten years past, and he had coveted this woman who looked at him with cool and assessing eyes. Arvid had seen it happen...a sort of nonphysical lust had taken control of the Commander.

He had wanted Lilias Strindberg as a possession, like the many others, male and female, that he was, even then, collecting in his Stronghold. The fact that she had chosen Liston Strindberg for her mate, long years since, and had borne him children who were now adults did not affect the Commander's intentions in the least.

When Lilias rejected his invitation to accompany him to Station, ostensibly as his nurse, she did it gently, as she did most things. This misled Standish into believing her to be pliable and easily overawed, although her son Arvid could have told him this was a fatal mistake. He tried to take liberties with her person, to prove to her that he was her master.

She broke his arm to match his collarbone, when he attempted to force her. Standish never forgot, and he never forgave. He had no experience with objects of his desire daring to resist, much less to injure him. When he recovered sufficiently to manage it, he returned to Tellich and gave the ruling Grange there an ultimatum.

They must outlaw all of Lilias's children, hang them if they caught them, and keep a price on their heads forever, if they were not captured. Otherwise Tellich would find no outlet for its grain, its vegetables, and its pork. The shuttle would be foreclosed to any produce from the area, and the goods the Traders left on the platform in exchange for their foodstuffs would be a thing of the past.

This included all replacement parts for any machinery or equipment manufactured off-world. In addition, he threatened to interdict the sophisticated medical supplies that those on the planet needed to keep them healthy. There was only one answer to give him. The Grange agreed, after Arvid, his sister, and his brother had sent word for them to do it. By that time, Lilias's brood and their families had taken to the woods.

Lilias and Liston disappeared with such thoroughness that not even the resources of Station had ever located them again. Standish had tried repeatedly to find the woman who dared to resist him, as Arvid had observed through his spies still living in the communities. A wounded ego was a matter the Commander's frail mental balance could not withstand.

It amused her son mightily to think that Lilias and her husband were now servants in the Stronghold, keeping watch on the man they both knew to be dangerous to their world. Healing was not the only art the herbalist knew; she had changed her appearance and that of Arvid's father so he would not recognize them, if he should see them again. No word had come to him from them in three years, yet Arvid knew with an inner certainty that they were still alive, and well and busy ferreting out secrets the Commander surely did not want known.

He stared again at Stormwall's sharp ridge. The sky was dark with cloud, and the wind was blowing sharply, even into this sheltered spot. An early fall seemed to be upon them, and probably a winter harsh enough to starve many and to make all of his people miserable and ill. That was the worst of living in the forest.

He sighed as he climbed down from the tree and stretched his cramped muscles. He had stayed aloft longer than he intended.

As he beckoned to Garet, his closest friend and lieutenant, motion was discernible among the bushes that fringed the wood on the north. Someone was approaching the forest, he knew with sudden certainty. That might signal danger for his people.

The four lookouts who had gathered there disappeared as if by magic, while Arvid and Garet dropped and crawled through the surrounding undergrowth to a point from which they could see the path leading into the wood. The forest's paths had been arranged with artful naturalness to seem untouched by human devices. Yet they placed the utmost difficulty in the way of anyone thinking to walk along any of them. The path leading in was deliberately arranged to give watchers a good view of anyone following it, while they remained unseen and unsuspected.

Arvid was able to see that those who came through the brush found the path with some ease and avoided the pitfalls without great difficulty. This told him they were no purblind folk of the villages, able to tread on a hornbeast without suspecting its presence. And they moved quietly, once they were past the thick-growing bushes that were tangled together with stickery vines.

When they came past the first of the many deep bends in the way, he saw, too, that they were women. One was youngish, square-built, walking with the easy tread of a person ready at any instant to repel an attack. The other was old, tiny...surely too fragile to risk herself in the forest with winter at her heels.

He glanced aside at Garet and quirked an eyebrow. These two seemed too innocent, too unthreatening. It had been his experience that nobody at all was as lacking in threat as the two women appeared. Whoever traveled at their heels, hoping to take advantage of the distraction they might cause, would be surprised. Fatally so.

He signaled with a trill that ended with the characteristic chirp of the graybeak warbler. A real bird took up the melody, making it unnecessary for him to contribute the second part of his message. As he watched, the two on the path were suddenly surrounded by men; there were only three, but they were so large and so bulky they seemed to envelop their quarry, instead of standing before and behind them.

The gray-brown homespun clothing the captors wore made them seem almost invisible. That was, Strindberg thought, the reason why those few who had ever escaped their clutches had told tales of being accosted by ghosts in Coldfellow Wood. Even as he rose to confront the newcomers, however, his thought was interrupted by the sudden disruption of the group on the path.

Valle, the biggest of the men, flew off the path and into a tangle of wirebush, landing with a crunch of branches and the ripping of cloth. The wirebush lived up to its name. Before he had completed his graceful arc, Carrick went backward into the vine-grown tangle and disappeared with a thump. So. One, at least, of these women was a warrior of great skill, if of little bulk. Even as Strindberg moved swiftly up the path, the third of his men sank onto the path, out cold.

"Be still, or you will die," he said, his voice cold as the wind that now whistled among the treetops.

The young woman turned on her heel, her hands moving toward her belt. He could not have said why he did not kill her, but he aimed his pellet weapon with quick precision, and she went down, stunned but not dead.

The old woman looked down at her companion, then up at him. She smiled grimly, and he saw in that instant her likeness to Theron Standish. He leaped over the fallen men, his bulk and weight forgotten, and struck her down where she stood. She crumpled at his feet, her white hair stained with blood that welled from a cut in her scalp. She looked like a broken toy, thrown away into the forest, and he felt a sudden surge of guilt.

Standish had many relatives on Granary—all the hundred and fifty thousand inhabitants were, perforce, the descendants of the original thousand colonists, planeted there a hundred generations before. There was no reason why anyone he met might not resemble the Commander.

"Blast my temper!" he muttered, as he bent to lift the almost weightless ancient. "She couldn't hurt me if she tried."

Garet caught up the other woman and kicked his fallen fellow, still lying amid the vines. "Up, you lazy beast," he said. "This woman sent you flying like skillballs into a net. What a comedown for the great Carrick, who wrestles six-legged predators for fun and attacks armies alone, according to your own accounts. Come along back to the Center with us. Arvid is going to want to talk with you."

Valle too, groaning in the middle of the wirebush, began to move. Additional rips told of his progress, as he extricated himself and stood once again on the path. "My head!" he moaned. "My back! What hit me?"

Garet began to shake with laughter. "Come along, oh great and terrible warrior. We will find the answer to that, among other things, when we reach the camp."

Arvid was going ahead, his long legs moving soundlessly through the ferns and vines that overhung the path, his big feet landing silently, carrying him and his burden toward the late summer encampment of his refugee people. He was thinking hard, moving automatically to avoid the pitfalls he had personally designed for the downfall of any approaching enemy.

Who were these women who had come alone to Coldfellow Wood? There was no one following them; his watchmen out in the brush would have whistled if there had been any sign of that. Why had two women come into his domain? If it were for treachery, he would be on guard. They would have no chance to betray his people to those who hunted them. And if not?

He would find the answer to that, if it required the truthweed to do it.

CHAPTER EIGHT

To Hold a Karmann Is Never Easy

Strindberg arrived at the seasonal camp far ahead of his fellows, and Nedra met him before the shelter they shared. She looked at the unconscious woman in his arms and caught her breath harshly.

"Who is that? And what have you done?" she asked, turning into the cramped space where she kept their supplies. "Put her here on the cot. There. Lay her flat while I get water and a cloth. She's bleeding badly."

"Scalp wounds do that," he said, trying to keep his tone undisturbed. He straightened the thin arms, the legs, the disarranged tunic and trousers. "This may be a spy from Standish's side of the fence. Or it may be someone trying something on behalf of the farmers. We'll see. If she's innocent, I'm sorry I hit her. But if she's a threat, she'll die."

Nedra stared at him, and he saw in her eyes the deep understanding they shared, even though she disagreed with his attitude. He had battled it out with himself long ago; one who is the hunted cannot afford mercy. Those who wanted his death would never rest, and he knew it; to take a chance was foolish.

"Is there truthweed in the stores?" he asked her, looking upward at the hanging bunches of herbs she gathered every summer against the needs of the winter.

Slowly, painfully, they were learning that Granary did, indeed, supply the medicinal needs of these newcomers and might, in time, replace the off-world cures that came scantily into Station. It would require generations of careful testing, since they had been cut off from the off-world supplies of the Stronghold, to find which were the things that worked and which the ones that killed.

She reached to take down a withered batch of leaves from

among others hanging in pairs from a brittle central stem. "I do not gather a great deal of it, but this should be enough to loose the tongues of this one and another, too. But handle it carefully."

"You keep cautioning me, but I know how dangerous it can be," he objected, taking the bunch and putting it into a fold of cloth that he deposited in his pocket. "How many captives have I killed with the stuff?"

"Too many," she said. "When they die after taking the dose, you learn nothing, and, innocent or guilty, you have sentenced them to death. You take proper care, or I will gather no more, and there is not another soul among your brainless crew who could tell a stickeryvine from a honey apple."

He sighed. Nedra was the perfect mate; she had followed him into exile without a whimper. She had reared their two daughters in the forest under far less than comfortable circumstances. Now her children were grown and leading small groups of their own, over the mountains in the uplands above Sterne Rift and Ellanish, she used her time wisely, nursing the sick, learning all she could about the effects of the herbs she gathered and tested (usually upon herself), and mastering the art of personal combat.

That last seemed to be a thing whose time was coming swiftly, and Arvid was glad she recognized the necessity before he must advise her to prepare for it. Now, however, she bent over the unconscious woman, more concerned for this possible enemy than Arvid liked for her to be. She had fought him, several times, over the killing of spies who had infiltrated their ranks, insisting he provide more proof than was possible in their circumstances.

He turned and left the room to check on the other captive. She had been taken directly to the compound reserved for those who must be held against their wills. There were more and more of those as Standish tried repeatedly to move his own agents into a position from which they could destroy the free people in the forest.

Only two ragged boys, still insisting they had hunted for lost goats, and an old man too addled to remember his name, were confined there at present. Arvid suspected the ancient was an informant sent by the Grange of Tellich, which had never given up its pro forma attempts to capture him and his siblings in order to ingratiate themselves with the Commander.

A thought made Strindberg pause in the middle of the path. If Standish now was attacking Tellich, would the ruling Grange, consisting of the most prominent landholders and the most efficient tenant farmers, still exist? And would they, if they did exist, still care about bringing his people to book? He shook his head to dislodge the illogical thought, and went to stare through the poles of the wooden cage that enclosed the prisoners. The square-faced woman he had stunned was holding her head in her hands, but she made no sound as she sat on the dried leaves heaped into one corner.

He could see the long muscles in her arms, where they emerged from the sleeves of her heavy wrap. The muscles of a fighter, without doubt. These women must have been sent either by Standish or by the President of the Grange!

Garet emerged from the hut he shared with his brother Garn. "She came around quickly, that one. A tough woman, I should say. She said nothing, but she looked holes through me when I put her into the cage. Do you have the truthweed?"

Arvid sighed. "Nedra gave me some, but you know how she feels about captives. We'll have to wait until everyone sleeps, tonight, before we question those two. My wife will be hard to live with, as it is, if we must kill them. If she has to watch us question them, she'll send me out into the forest to sleep with the wolves."

Garet laughed, understanding. "You live with a she wolf," he said. "Some envy you her strength and loyalty, but not one envies you her tongue."

They went to find Valle and Carrick, who had sought out the medic to tend their various cuts and abrasions. Neither was kindly disposed toward either of the captive women. They agreed it would be best to question the pair after the camp went to its rest, using persuasion, if that would suffice, truthweed if not. And a judicious beating, Valle observed, never did any woman much harm anyway.

Arvid thought of what would happen if he ever tried beating Nedra, and shuddered. A knife in the gut would be the least of his punishments, he guessed.

The other women, less than half of the complement in the forest, were tough as well, ill-disposed toward any male who raised an intemperate hand toward them. There was no tradition of abuse of women or children among his people, though sometimes he was tempted to try it. Tonight, in fact, something of the sort would be a possibility.

* * * * * * *

Seleva woke and stared up into a darkness striped with distant firelight. The roof above her was patched with reddish flickers, as the light found its way between the laths and strips forming the walls of the place in which she lay.

She tried to recall just what had happened, but her principal impression was that of a huge shape leaping toward her. Nothing but darkness followed that recollection. She tested out her limbs, her muscles, feeling the familiar aches and cramps that had come with age, but also enduring a dreadful throbbing in her head.

She reached to touch her face, but her hands were tied before her with strips of soft cloth. Her ankles were similarly bound. She wriggled to the side of the narrow cot on which she lay and moved her legs off the edge, forcing her body upright as she sat.

Now she could see out between the poles at eye level. A watch-fire bloomed in the middle of a small clearing. She could see firelit branches overhanging the spot. That should hide it from the air by day, if not in darkness. Good planning, she thought, as she tried to see through the murk.

There were huts around the clearing, each tucked beneath a huge tree. Again, good thinking had prevailed. Though she could not see any of them clearly, she suspected they were all temporary construction like the one in which she sat, made to come down hurriedly and to be moved through the forest to another campsite.

As she watched, someone strode across the clearing and spoke to an invisible watchman beyond her field of vision. She thought it must be the big man who had struck her...this one walked with the same bear-like gait, agile and swift for one so large. He looked as if he might be coming toward her.

She felt for the small silver ornament at her waist. It was still there, and she sighed with relief. It looked like an inexpensive bauble, the sort that people tend to wear for sentimental reasons. The leads that went through the leather of her belt to make contact with her own skin and nerves were so unobtrusive that a casual observation would never reveal anything unusual about the thing.

Seleva pressed her elbow inward against the button. A jolt of horrifying agony surged through her, making her adrenals kick in, her heart speed up, her mind sharpen into instant focus. And, in that moment of augmented awareness, she realized something important. She smiled as the door was pushed open and the burly man stepped inside.

It took a moment for him to realize she was sitting; he had been out in the firelight, and his eyes required a bit of adjustment. He inhaled quickly when he saw her at last. "You are awake...that is good," he said. "We are going to join your friend, outside. Here, let me cut loose your feet." A quick motion with his knife set her ankles free, and she moved them, stretching and flexing her toes so their numbness would not make her fall when she stood again.

"Come on. My friends are waiting for us." He caught her under the elbow and pulled her upright, where she swayed for an instant on her tingling feet. Then she could walk, and she was propelled ahead of her captor as he crossed the firelit space again, and pushed her into the shelter of a thick stand of smaller trees. She halted when his hand moved away from her arm. Although she still swayed a bit, she found her balance and stood waiting.

"Valle! Do you have her?"

There came a string of curses, which told Seleva that Lemmon had made a fight of it, and a frantic rustle of movement told her the troopmistress had not yet given it up. Another voice came from the shadows. "She bit him good, then kicked him where it hurts the most. Old Valle won't be the man he was for quite a while."

"Close your mouth, you brainless fool!" said the first voice. "Yes, I have her. Come and get it over with before I kill her, Arvid. Whoever taught this one to fight did a real job of it."

Arvid pulled Seleva into the thicket, and she felt the slender branches, still leafy in this sheltered spot, whip about her ears. Then she stood in the center of a tiny space lit by a dim lanthorn in which a candle burned.

Lemmon lay against a stone beyond the light, her hands tied and her dark eyes blazing with fury. They had neglected to tie her feet down to something solid, and Seleva guessed she had begun kicking wickedly when her captors were distracted by the approach of the big man.

Seleva nodded to her reassuringly, though she knew Lemmon could have no idea of the weapon she had at her command. The men who crouched on either side of her looked somewhat the worse for wear, their scratches and bruises from the first encounter now being augmented by a black eye, a hand that dripped blood from a severe bite, and a pronounced tendency on the part of Valle to favor his lower torso. The old woman almost chuckled aloud, no matter how badly her head was pounding.

"You have wasted your time and energy," Seleva said, her tone quiet and quite calm. "We came to you from General Coville, who commands the remnant of troops under the very last of the Grange-masters of Tellich, Shemyona Fenn. We came to make a truce with you, so those who survived Stormwall may travel through the forest to the hills and the mountains beyond."

She turned to stare far up into Arvid Strindberg's shadowed eyes. "Surely you are not so stupid or so removed from what passes in the countryside around you as to doubt that Theron Standish is your enemy!"

The man looked as immovable as Sterne Rift itself. He shook

his head. "All are our enemies, the Grange of Tellich not the least of them. And if Shemyona Fenn is the last of the Council, good riddance to them all. Do you expect us to believe that all of those are gone and only Fenn is left to direct this country? An unlikely tale. And you...you look too much like Standish himself to be any but blood kin. Why should we believe you?"

Seleva drew herself upright. "I am Seleva Karmann, grandmother of the Commander of Station. I am my grandson's most determined enemy, though I hope to reform, not to kill, my misguided descendant. The time has come, Arvid Strindberg, when you must trust someone, however unlikely that may have seemed to you as recently as yesterday.

"Coville will bring his wounded and his fit troops through the northern edge of Coldfellow Wood within hours. Will you add to his losses by trying to prevent that?"

"And what are you doing with the forces of Tellich?" Strindberg asked her. "You belong in safety in Station."

"I have come to collect...energy." She smiled grimly. "I will take what I gather home to my grandson and make him suffer the things he has imposed upon his innocent and guilty people."

She turned abruptly and forced the button at her belt against Strindberg's bulky thigh. The man shrieked, dropping to his knees with his hands clasped over the spot where contact had been made. His skin turned bluish with shock, as his fellows stared at him in astonishment.

Valle and Carrick leaped to their feet and looked down at their incapacitated leader. Arvid groaned, still holding his thigh in both hands. Seleva knelt, caught up the knife out of his sling, and severed her bonds. When she stood, she turned to face the two startled men.

"That is what I feel, every time I charge my weapon. I suffer every death, every wound, every ill that takes place while the device is activated. I can transfer the pain through the device itself or by merely touching you with my finger while pressing down the button. So take care how you approach me. You may not want to suffer what your leader is enduring."

Arvid forced himself to stand, though he listed toward the painful leg even as he held himself upright. The bag holding the truthweed hung, forgotten, from his belt loop. "You feel that? Constantly?"

"No, of course not. I could do nothing but lie flat and shriek, if that were true. I feel it as I gather it. When I begin to falter, I give myself a jolt to get my aged nerves and muscles into motion again.

"But do not waste our time upon such foolish questions. Will you allow our people to pass through Coldfellow Wood?" She felt the time ticking away now, faster and faster. The refugees from Stormwall would, even at this hour, be approaching the scrubland beyond the northern reaches of the wood.

Strindberg turned and stared into the eyes of his henchmen. All were dim and shadowy, for the candle had burned low in the lanthorn, and its light was quivering, preparatory to going out entirely. Seleva stood silent, waiting, until the leader turned again to her. "We will watch them, do not doubt it. If there is treachery here, many will die. But they may pass. We will clear a path—only one for them to use."

Seleva nodded with satisfaction. "When you take the time to think, you will see there is no motive for treachery now. We must pass. We must be gone before Standish's flying troops soar over Stormwall, dropping death onto its height. He traded, some time ago, for a number of the flying machines, and he found a deserter from the Traders' militia to teach his people to use them."

Strindberg went very still, and she could see him thinking of all the possibilities for disaster the use of flying forces might pose for his own people, now camped so near to Stormwall. She nodded with satisfaction.

"You would do well to move your camp," she said. "You have hidden your homes well, but who knows what some sharp-eyed youngling may see, as he passes overhead?"

The pain seemed to be subsiding, for Strindberg was standing straighter, forgetting about his leg as he stared down at her. "You are truly his grandmother? And you intend to stop him?"

She nodded again, her hair shining white in the last of the firelight. "I am a Karmann. We do what we must. But do not expect to keep us captive for long...we are most resistant to the idea of imprisonment."

She moved to Lemmon's side and cut her bonds. "Can you find Coville in the darkness?" she asked. "We must get word to him soon."

Lemmon stood and stretched her cramped muscles. "I can. Good work, Madame Karmann. I will tell the General you will join us...where?"

"I will meet you beyond the wood, at Phantom Hill," she said. "This large man is going to show me a short way to reach my goal, for I am old and tired and my legs protest. Go with luck, Lemmon. I will see you soon."

Strindberg was staring down at her with astonishment, but her assurance was so complete that when she gestured for him to go, he turned at once toward the east. She could see protest in the set of his heavy shoulders, but he did not turn to argue with her.

She followed him into the wood. Valle and Carrick, dumb with wonder, came behind, their big feet silent upon the age-old mulch of the forest floor, as they headed up and up through the foothills into the high country.

CHAPTER NINE

THE SLAVE OF STATION

Yace heaved, and the wagon quivered minutely, even though the draft animals were leaning into the harness, and three more of his fellows were giving it all they had, pushing mightily. Even as he felt his tendons cracking, the whip cracked even more sharply.

He felt its metal-tipped thong curl around his back, licking nastily at his shoulder. Blood joined the mud sliming down his ribs, and he breathed deeply to keep his temper under control. If Jarek could provoke him into open rebellion, that would be the excuse the brute needed to kill him, without fear of retaliation from the officers in charge of the post controlling this part of Ellanish.

And Jarek wanted to kill him. He and Yace had been at daggers' points since they were children. The hulking son of the overseer who directed farming on the Grange's common cropland bullied every child in the group. Only Yace stood up to him at every opportunity, managing to hold his own, if never to win any of their fights.

Both had been whipped more times than Yace could count by parents, teachers, overseers, and random adults who objected to the commotion they always seemed to arouse. They had been shuttled into the cooperative pea fields as soon as they reached the age of twelve, principally in order to keep them from disrupting classes in the Grange's school. Jarek had hated him ever since, for while the big boy was no scholar, he hated hard work even more than he did study.

When Standish invaded Ellanish, it had not surprised Yace that his old enemy turned traitor and joined the enemy forces. Treachery insured him a job on the right end of the whip, while his family and his peers were enslaved. Now he scowled down from his seat in the wagon, curling the whip again for another cut at the men straining below.

The team of beasts pulling the wagon was not made up of horses that his ancestors had brought as fertilized ova to Granary, but of animals bred from the original stock. They had been adapted to this new world with the help of some genetic manipulation on the part of one of the technically oriented worlds in the Cooperative. They were bigger, heavier, their heads shaped strangely, and their eyes bright and knowing, though few of Yace's people admitted that their draught beasts were, in many cases, as intelligent as they were.

Now the animals put their broad backs into pulling, as their splayed hooves bit into the muck. The wheels sucked in the sticky mud, and the wagon bed groaned. The efforts of the united men and beasts began to have some effect, for the tall wheels moved an inch, two inches, then an entire foot up the slope of the stream's eastern bank. Yace heaved again, his whipcord body tensed with stress, his muscles standing out like ropes from the leathery skin of his arms and back. Every day he worked in the transport of the Commander's crop requisitions he grew stronger, he knew.

One day he would find himself strong enough to attack Jarek, and that would be the time when he went free into the mountains to the west, among the forested slopes and the stone faces of the peaks. He would leave Jarek dead or castrated, which might be an even more suitable punishment. Even in his present misery he almost smiled at the thought.

The vehicle went up the bank amid a shower of watery mud from the wheels, and the exhausted men staggered out after it, wiping sweat from their foreheads onto smeared forearms. Jarek, frustrated that the task had been completed so soon, laid the whip across them again, forcing them to run ahead of the blundering wagon and the tired beasts.

Even as he dashed past the team, Yace noticed a glint in the eye of the nearer of the animals. In the instant of contact, he felt there was sympathy in the beast's gaze. The animal had an easier life in every way than did he, in the grip of the Commander's forces.

Then he was past, running down the graveled way toward the military post, to which the wagon load of vegetables and grain was headed. A group of men in camouflage uniforms was already lined up, ready to unload in a hurry and to send the slaves back for another shipment.

That told Yace something; they had never been in so much of a hurry before this. Food had not been of great interest to them, for this was a food-producing world, more fertile than any in the entire Consortium, the rare trace elements in its soil keeping the Traders healthy in their unnatural environment of ship life.

What had made the difference? Had some element in the war beyond the mountains changed to alter the balance of control over the fields and the harvest that was just now being completed before the fall storms blew in from the northwest. If battles raged across the fields, or the fire weapons destroyed them, there would be hunger in places like Station, which did not grow more than a fraction of their own food.

He was thinking so hard he missed Jarek's order to fall in line with the soldiers and pass the bags and bundles along. A snap of the whip, just grazing his cheek, brought him to attention, and he heaved a sack of cornmeal along to the nearest man in the line. Another half inch would have seen his eyeball burst under the impact of the metal tip.

The man beside him was a slight, worried-looking individual whose uniform fitted him badly. He staggered under the weight of the bag, but he managed to pass it to the man beyond him. He shrugged, as Yace offered him another, but there was a hint of fellow feeling in his washed-out gray eyes.

They worked in silence until the wagon was empty. Then Jarek jumped down from the seat and followed the officer in charge into his office to get a receipt and further orders. That gave the unsoldierly-looking trooper a chance to squat beside Yace and chance a whisper.

"You look fit, still. Most of the others are just about out of it," he said softly. "Are you game for something dangerous?"

Yace pretended to be drawing idly in the dust. YES formed beneath his dirty finger, as he said, equally quietly, "When you will be dead within six months, what can seem dangerous?"

The skinny fellow turned half away, as if resting against the wagon wheel for a short doze. His gruff voice floated over his shoulder to Yace's ears. "Things go badly for the Commander in the west. I have heard Stormwall was defended well, and the Station lost men and equipment that cannot be replaced."

Yace yawned, scratched, and grunted, rising as Jarek and the officer returned. Jarek did not look happy.

"You must move all the stores to our sheds. They are no longer secure in the barns. We must have them here, guarded by many men with efficient weapons instead of by a handful of farmers with pellet guns and sticks," the officer was insisting, as they came up.

That sounded encouraging. So there were rebels on this side of the mountains, were there? He turned enough to nod at the thin soldier. The man passed him, brushing against him as he did so.

Yace found a paper thrust into his shirt, where the buttons were missing. He shrugged, making the note slip down into a secure position, and took his place in the wagon.

The orders were specific: they were to move at top speed on the return journey, making as many trips as possible for as long as the light lasted. Once night fell, the job must wait, for the night, even this far from the forests on the slopes of the mountains, held carnivores. Not all the efforts of the farmers for generations had succeeded in making the valley's woodlands more than relatively safe in the hours of darkness. Beasts of many kinds roamed there, most of them dangerous to human beings.

While slaves were expendable, the draft animals were not. So Jarek whipped them into a trot, jouncing the wagon along the chuckholes in the graveled road, while the wind off the mountains picked up both strength and chill. The men huddled in the back of the vehicle held onto anything possible, their backsides wearing through the skimpy flesh left on them, as the board bottom of the wagon tried to batter them flat.

Now the sweat had dried, and the wind off the snowfields of the heights was cutting through them, for their clothing was a choice collection of rags inadequate for warmth. Yace huddled against the men before and behind him, though that meant bumped heads and bruised elbows when the wheels dropped into holes or jerked over big rocks in the road. He even managed to doze a bit, though his nightmares almost came up out of the depths to haunt him.

A particularly evil jolt woke him fully, and he fell to thinking about the soldier back at the post. What had he meant to imply, with his hints and his sly looks? Was there some revolt afoot among the Commander's own troops? Or was this man an agent of those who resisted the invasion of Ellanish?

Jarek gave a shout, and Yace looked ahead. The sun was half down the sky, and the barns were in sight, with a group of men waiting to help load their contents into the wagon. Again and again, they would make this trip, struggling through deeper mud every time, as they crossed the stream with the loaded wagon.

They would make one more, he thought, before night was too near to risk. That would put them in the post overnight. Perhaps it would give him a chance to talk with the skinny soldier without risking Jarek's attentive eye. It would not do to be discovered conspiring against the Commander. That had happened, in the past month.

He could still see the quivering shape of the man tied to the post, the flash of the knife blade as Jarek ran it along his legs and arms. The taint of blood in sunlight lingered in his nostrils. He still heard the shrieks that accompanied drawing off the victim's skin, inch by inch, as Jarek peeled it away like flexible clothing from the agonized limbs and the jerking torso. When he was done, the thing left looked nothing like a man.

Yace did not intend to risk that fate, though he knew Jarek would love to treat him with equal tenderness. But he would—of course he would—find the chance to ask what the gray-eyed man had meant. There was more to his hints than the simple need to communicate. Something behind his eyes had promised greater things to come.

Yace climbed down from the wagon, stretched his stiff and aching muscles, and once again began to heave foodstuff into its capacious bed. Perhaps things were not as hopeless as they had seemed, since his country had fallen to Station.

CHAPTER TEN

TWO TALKS IN DARKNESS

The slaves were quartered in a shed half filled with empty grain bags. It was not uncomfortable; indeed, compared with the quarters Jarek usually found for his men, it was positively luxurious. But Yace did not allow that to lull him into a deep sleep. As soon as the others were snoring and groaning in their chosen places, he slid silently toward the door, which was made of rough lumber hinged at the top. He slipped under it without opening it out more than a foot and stood for a moment, letting his eyes get used to the darkness.

Hakle, the man he was to meet, was a slick one. He had given Yace directions so subtly nobody present had any inkling of what he was doing. He'd worked in the time ("When the Ten Sisters go over the mountain") and the place ("Beyond the fence around the latrine") among his constant groanings and gripings as they worked. The lieutenant in charge of the troop had called him down repeatedly for making so much noise, but Hakle seemed to be considered a necessary nuisance. He certainly was not the best worker in the troop.

Yace looked up at the rim of mountains to the west. The Ten Sisters, stars clumped closely into an irregular oval, were just sliding out of sight beyond a ragged peak. It was time to move, and he worked his way on bare soles through the post, avoiding the graveled paths. He could smell the latrine long before he came to it.

The walls of the latrine bulked against the lighter shading of the parade ground stretching beyond it. The fence was a welcome barrier, and he stooped and went around it until it met the wall surrounding the post itself. Out of sight, he felt much more secure, and he paused to whistle faintly. A perfectly rendered night cry of the Rufous Singing Night Crake answered his call. He sighed and sat on the ground, as footsteps approached him.

"Hakle," came the whisper as another sat beside him. "And I have news."

Yace felt his heart begin to thud more quickly. The tone the man used seemed unaccountable. "Well, tell me," he whispered, to cover his excitement.

"There's a bunch coming over the mountains. Wounded and experienced troops are staying in the high country, hidden in the caverns there. Some of those warriors from Tellich are going to slip down into the fields of Ellanish and burn the stores the Commander is counting on to see his people through the winter. They've already sent scouts to get in touch with the sleepers among the troops here."

"And what about the slaves?" asked Yace. "What do we do?"

"Escape," came the reply. "What ones have the energy left...and the nerve."

Yace tried to see his face, but it was too dark, there in the shelter of the walls. The starlight was too dim to help any.

"When?" he asked.

"Tonight, as soon as possible. Tomorrow, they'll all know there's trouble coming, and things will tighten up. The first fires are going to be set tonight; there's no need for your boss to go back for another load. It won't be there. If you're loose, you may be able to do some good. But if you're shackled with these half-dead creatures, you might as well die and be done with it."

Yace drew a careful breath. The thought of escaping from the years of field work, the last months of slavery under Jarek's whip, the entire notion of living under the iron rule of the Commander, filled him with something near to intoxication.

"Now?" he breathed. Beyond the latrine, in the compound, the watch was changing, boots crunching on gravel, low voices speaking briefly. In a few minutes, he would be able to run, if all went well.

"Now," said Hakle. "This wall behind us is unscalable any place else. But the latrine wall joins it right above our heads. You can climb onto that from the door, there. Hoist yourself on that, that's right. Now balance and walk the top—just like that!—and there you are, waist high to the outer wall.

"Good luck, Yace! And carry word to anybody you see that this country is going up in flames in the next few weeks. Tell them to get busy...help is on the way!"

Yace stared down into blackness beyond the barrier. The brush had been cut away to a depth of several yards, but he knew there might be stubble that would ruin his feet, if he leaped down. He caught the top of the wall and let his feet down, hanging, at last, by his hands. When he let go he dropped only his own height or a bit less.

He thought regretfully of the remnants of his boots, which still rested beside his pile of grain bags. But freedom was worth sore feet, he reflected, as he moved away into the line of low shrubs and small trees beyond the cleared space. He had nothing, being a slave, and so he was not tied to a place by possessions. Perhaps those who were tied so were the sorriest slaves of all....

Even as he thought that, the sky far to the west began to glow. Dimly at first, then more and more brightly the flame bloomed, until the sky was red and angry-looking. The clouds that hung down the sides of the mountains glowed red-gold. Behind him he heard the alert signal sounded on the pipe the watchman carried, and he ran through the tangle of brush and trees, leaving shreds of his clothing behind him. That would not lead anyone to him, he felt sure. They would be too busy saving the food that would hold off starvation for the coming winter. They were all going to run hell for leather for the barns, where the winter's stores were awaiting transfer to the post. When hunger looked them in the eyes, few of those troopers or officers or even Jarek himself were going to think to count the slaves who went along to help fight the blaze.

He ran, before he knew what was happening, out over the brink of a stream, a branch of the one to the west, which he had not expected to find quite so quickly, and went splashing into a deep eddy. He went down like a rock, unprepared, with no breath held in his lungs. He struggled upward mightily, his eyeballs feeling as if they might pop from his face, and at last he surfaced with a splash and a whoosh of breath.

As he cleared the water from his ears and eyes with a shake of the head, he found he could hear shouts in the distance. Even from his position between the tall banks of the stream, he could see a glare against the sky where the grain barns burned.

He found himself wondering why the troops from Tellich had crossed the mountains to make their attacks here in Ellanish. Everyone knew Tellich was, as yet, unconquered. Surely they stood a better chance of stopping the Commander on their own ground. Or had some catastrophe driven them across the mountains to Ellanish?

He waded ashore, still thinking hard. Unless, of course, they intended to draw off a goodly part of the Station forces to fight this threat, allowing still another group of the rebels, left in Tellich, to push and harry whatever forces were left on their own soil.

The breeze was cold on his wet skin, and his rags hung, soggy and chilled, against him. There was, he knew, a house to the west. It had belonged, before the Commander's incursion, to a friend of his father. Now it had been allotted to one of the traitors who had made the Station's attack on Ellanish so easily won. The farm his own family had worked on a rental basis for generations had been allotted to just such a turncoat.

Yace sneezed violently, feeling the night breeze fingering through his wet clothing. It was find shelter or get pneumonia, he knew, for this was the herald of the first cold wind of fall.

The traitor in that nearby house had died mysteriously, there on his stolen property, and as far as Yace knew the place stood empty. It would shelter him from the wind. He had lived for too long in this country to risk pneumonia, if he could help it. He made for the path he had walked so many times as a boy, when he followed his father on visits.

Durk had been his chum. The son of Darrell, his father's friend, and he had been almost as close as brothers, and often they met at the stream to fish. By night and by day, he had passed along the worn game tracks, brushing through the layered leaves of many autumns. There was something comforting, even in his present circumstances, in following that old way. Even his chill, now that he was moving briskly, was subsiding, for his blood warmed with exercise.

He paused as a hornbeast crashed away through the thickly grown trees. He waited until the sounds died away in the distance, but before he could get his legs into motion again he heard behind him the sound of cautious feet on the dusty path. Someone was behind him, probably intending to bring him back into the hands of Jarek again.

Yace breathed out, very slowly and silently, as he sidled into the undergrowth and slipped to his knees. Whoever it might be could not know where, exactly, he was. If it looked possible, he would wring the man's neck. If it did not, he would remain still and quiet, as did the animals, letting the blunderer go past and search for him where he did not intend to go.

It was dark, even in the open. Within the forest it was pitchy, and the constant scraping and chirring of the late autumn insects tended to cover any sound. But he could hear, once he focused his ears upon the task, the feet coming nearer and nearer. He even heard the scratching of thorn vines against cloth and quickly indrawn breath told him the claw-like stickers had drawn blood.

Yace's eyes, always good, had adjusted to the darkness enough to distinguish between shades of blackness. A darker blot passed between his position and the faintly lighter bole of the big tree beyond the path. It was a much shorter, slighter shadow than his own, and he lunged, without taking time to think, to catch it about the knees and bring it to earth.

He was on top of the struggling bundle before it could do more than squeak, holding it down as he searched for the neck. When his calloused fingers closed about it, he stopped, thinking furiously. This neck was thin, fragile, the throat of a child or a woman. The heartbeat beneath his hands was frantic, thready, frighteningly unsteady.

He lay atop the warm shape and whispered, "Who are you? Why are you following me?"

The body went still for a long moment. Then a hesitant voice, childishly shrill, said, "I be Jon. The soldiers, they went to see the fire, and I got away over the wall. A man helped me, and he said there was some'un else ahead could show me where to go and what to do. So I came. You kill me?"

Yace sighed and rose to his knees, helping the boy up. "You scared the living wits out of me, youngling. I thought it was one of those triple-damned soldiers, come to take me back. How did you keep from getting wet?"

The boy snickered softly. "Jon knows about the woods. Jon got ways to cross. Rope hung in tree, it was still strong, and I swung over. But you wet. Better get dry, or you be sick."

"Exactly what I was thinking," Yace muttered. "Come with me, and walk carefully. There's a house up ahead, and it may or may not be empty."

He went forward, smelling the night, feeling the dry chill of the air, trying to feel ahead of them toward the house that should be standing empty. It might easily hold enemies instead.

The boy now moved far more quietly than before, and more than once Yace paused to make sure he still followed. At the last stop, one bend before the path entered the back garden of the house he sought, he whispered, "What did you do? For the soldiers?" To his surprise, the boy winced visibly.

The young voice was hard, even though the lad spoke softly. "I be there for the ones that don't like women. There be men I will kill, before I grow up."

Yace shuddered. He had no quarrel with men who loved men, but those who abused children he hated passionately. They had not been unheard of, even in Ellanish, where they were hanged quickly and without fanfare. He knew that in Station, with its greater leisure and wealth, many men had turned their wants toward the unproductive way. There were tales of children bought and sold like toys, and evidently the soldiery had brought those indulging in such cruel pastimes into the countryside.

"I'll help, if you want," he murmured. "But now you wait here in the edge of the wood, while I scout forward. The house is dark, but it's very late. There may be someone there. I'll make the click of a rock beetle if it's clear."

Jon tugged at his sleeve in reply, and Yace heard him sink into the deep ferns that bordered the garden. His breathing sounded ragged, and there was the hint of a wheeze when he inhaled.

Yace turned his steps toward the wide porch surrounding the house. There was a way to go beneath the structure into the storage place for wood. If he could gain that, he knew how to find the access shaft, up which the heavy logs were lifted to the waiting fireplace. He had helped Durk with that task more than once.

Once inside, he knew the rooms as well as his own father's house. Soon he would know if anyone was there. And then? He shook himself quietly as he moved on, wondering how he could find a way to safeguard the boy while finding the rebels and joining their forces. One step at a time, he thought. One step at a time. And then he was beneath the overhang of the porch, and it was so dark he must use every bit of every sense he possessed, in order to find the scuttle he was seeking.

CHAPTER ELEVEN

The Burglar Trade

If it had been dark outside, the situation inside the low doorway leading to the woodstore was beyond description. Yace could almost feel the thick, syrupy blackness against his face...and then he realized what he felt was cobwebs, draped in voluminous folds cross the narrow space.

He counted his steps, after raking away the sticky filaments, recalling the many games of hide and seek and pirate treasure he and Durk had played here on rainy days. Twenty steps—translating that from a child's short steps to a man's longer ones, he made it more like seventeen and he should be beside the lift that served the shaft.

Counting silently, he moved forward, steadying himself with a hand on the brick wall to his right. And at sixteen steps he felt the angle that marked the slot, down which the lift worked. The thing was like a chimney, built onto the side of the chimneystack, and the hatch leading into it was shut. He pried at the catch, finding it stuck after years of disuse. The old man who was Durk's father had lacked the strength to store great stacks of wood beneath his house, in later years after Durk had left for Station. He'd put what he gathered on his porch, for easier access.

Yace found himself wishing he had taken time from his work in the fields to help Darrell in the fall, when the wood must be gathered. He would have kept the old system in working order, and now he would have had a much easier time of it. He sighed. The laziness of youth was something that everyone, he supposed, had to outgrow or to have snatched from him. There was nothing like endless labor for the benefit of others, without hope of rest or gain, to make you appreciate what you used to have.

He felt about for the woodhook that used to hang just there! It was in place, crusty with rust, but still strong. He set the curved point in the crack beside the catch and pried briskly. There was a sharp snap, and the hatch sprang open, releasing a cloud of dust.

Yace began sneezing again, and it took some time for the dust clogging his head to clear enough to allow him to proceed. He opened the hatch again, for he had pushed it to, in order to keep the resounding sneezes from being piped up into the house. He knew how the shaft carried such things; he and Durk had learned many secrets by listening at its bottom as the men discussed their lives and their business before the fireplace.

The air rushed down toward him cool but not cold. There was a hint of wood smoke—not old smoke, but fresh. There must be people up there, he decided. What sort they might be was the thing he must learn.

He had a problem fitting his larger frame into the shaft, but after a time he had his shoulders wedged against the back, his knees against the front, and he caterpillared his way upward as he and his chum had done, years before. There in the darkness, with his youth risen freshly before his inner eye, he thought of his rebellious ways. What a waste!

If he had only been cooperative, he could have stayed on his father's farm, working to produce the specialized vegetables and fruits the old man had excelled at growing. Instead, he had toiled in the pea fields, to whose acres every farmer in the community contributed seed or fertilizer or labor or water for irrigation.

And he could have avoided the constant conflict with Jarek. He grinned suddenly into the blackness. Like Jon, he had scores to settle before he grew much older, and the cover of the rebel raid promised to give him the chance.

His head bumped against something above the upper end of the shaft, which was closed off with solid brick. At his right elbow, there was a soft thud against wood. He reached across himself to open this catch, hoping it would be easier than the first. His left hand was not going to do as well as his right had done, particularly in this cramped position.

There came a grating squeak, which seemed terribly loud in this confined space, but was, he knew, much less obvious outside it. The vent above it, which let air circulate down the shaft so those working below would not be stifled, gave a soft sigh as the opening door pulled in more air than usual.

Yace didn't move. He waited, listening intently for any sound, any indication that someone might have heard any of his movements. The dark silence did not stir. There was only the sound of a cricket someplace in the paneling, playing its farewell concert of the fall.

Now the time had come, he found he was not nearly so eager to search through the rooms of this once-familiar house. Even if no enemy slept there, memories would inhabit every one, waiting to ambush him as he opened each door. Durk, long gone into the city at Station. Darrell, dead these many months since he was dispossessed of his farm and his home. Lidia, who was a faint and pleasant memory of sweets at holiday time, and a comforting shoulder against which a small boy might weep away his real or imagined woes.

Worst of all, his own father would wait for him in the room they had always used when visiting overnight. The scent of the herbs Lidia had used on their bedding, the faint aroma of his father's skin, which mingled clean air and wood chips and fresh soil and something else that was uniquely Loran Engel...that might well greet him when he cracked that familiar door.

The calluses the months of slavery had formed around Yace's heart felt on the point of cracking away, leaving only the furious and terrified nineteen-year-old who had been hauled from the pea fields and into the service of the Commander's troops. Yace felt tender and sore, as if just up after a long illness.

He shook himself straight, once inside the invisible room, and put both hands to his head. This was no time to go soft. He must be ready to kill, without hesitation and without remorse, at any moment. He must be ready to die, if the necessity arose, taking with him anyone he could.

His bare foot clenched when he stepped off the braided rug by the fireplace onto the smooth hardwood floor, which was colder than he had expected. But bare feet went quietly, and he moved past the wide door to the kitchen, past the hall leading to the room where the composting toilet provided both convenience and topsoil, and to the foot of the stair.

Up there waited five large bedrooms, in any or all of which he might well find his death waiting. But dreading was not doing, as his father had always told him. He knew every step to avoid, as he went up the stair, and his accustomed feet knew which to tread on at the edge and which near the riser, in order to keep from making any one of them squeak. Before he was ready, he was at the top, peering down the dark hallway, trying to see those doors.

The first was to his left, just around the corner formed by the stairwell. He waited for a bit, listening hard, outside the closed door. Then, his hand light as a falling leaf, he touched the latch, pressed down, and pushed open the panel. He did not go inside. This had been Lidia and Darrell's room, and he had not entered it since she died.

He listened, knowing just what to detect if any living being slept in the room. There was no breath, however light, no slightest sound of a sleeper's unconscious motions. He slid inside and approached the spot where the bed had been. His knee touched the edge, and he let his hand drift downward, to touch a bare ticking, a tumble of covers. No warmth showed anyone had slept there recently.

He sighed, letting out the breath quietly, realizing only then how tense he had been. This was no easy job he had taken for himself. But it must be done, or he might wake in the morning enslaved again, subject to the demands of the likes of Jarek.

One by one, he tried the doors, found them unsecured from inside, and tested the rooms and the beds. Some of the couches were made, as if ready for a sleeper, but the bedclothes felt damp and smelled musty. He felt they had not been used since Gorel, the traitor who had claimed this holding as his reward from Standish, had died in this house.

The last door was at the end of the corridor. He had a strong feeling, as he neared it, that someone slept behind it. He was quieter than ever as he crept to try the latch. It too was unsecured from within.

He pushed slowly, and the panel opened enough to let him enter. He moved just inside, listening, listening, but he could hear no breath, though every instinct that he had told him someone was very near, surely alive and alert.

There was no sound. The breeze outside could not penetrate the heavy walls with its thin whine. He relaxed a bit and moved toward the spot where the bed had been, when last he had slept there with his father.

The door slammed with the sound of a snapping board. Something flipped about his neck, taking him off-balance and bringing him to his knees. A blade, razor sharp, touched the side of his neck, and a voice breathed into his ear, "Move and you die!"

CHAPTER TWELVE

ROUGH JOURNEY

Seleva was again tramping over rough ground at the heels of someone whose legs were far longer than her own. The wind, which had become even colder, whipped off Stormwall, through the forest, and bit through her jacket and gloves, making her wrist joints ache.

This was no weather for beginning a long journey...not for anyone. But it was a journey she must make. Ahead of her, Carrick stumbled over a rotted log, which had sunk deeply into the leaf mold. She paused gratefully, as he picked himself up and felt about with his stick, trying to find another obstacle before he went forward.

She took the opportunity to ask, "How far yet to Phantom Hill?"

Strindberg, behind her, didn't answer. He had not started off again but was standing still. Seleva realized he was listening hard. She closed her lips and listened, too, past the whisper of the chill wind in the needles of the conifers now replacing the hardwoods of the lower forest. And she heard something that turned her skin crinkly with dread.

A great cat, one of the most dangerous predators of Granary, was roaring, and the sound, almost inaudible at first, was growing louder and louder. The beast had scented them. That ill-fated wind had carried their scent to it, evidently, and it was anticipating a pre-dawn meal of man flesh. Seleva put her hand to the sling from which she suspended her pellet gun. A quick check, now easy even in the darkness, reassured her: it was still pumped up, with ammunition in the tube attached to the underside of the cylinder.

The small slug might weigh only a bit under an ounce, but the velocity the air pressure in the cylinder could attain was tremendous. A man or a small cat was easy prey...but one of the big cats clung to life tenaciously and fought to the end. Carrick hefted his metal-headed staff, and Seleva could hear Valle stringing his bow, the soft twang as the wood took up the slack of the gut sounding clearly, somewhere between the treble of the wind and the deep bass of the animal's growl. Seleva felt Strindberg push her between the pair, as they went on for a step or two.

Then, "Down!" shouted Valle, and she heard the swift rush of paws over dead leaves, the panting of great lungs. She smelled the ammoniac odor of the big beast, even as she plunged, face down, into a tumble of leaf-drift. She rolled quickly and had her pellet gun ready for anything that might come.

But Carrick's spear-like staff held the creature away. The sky, turning from black to gray, showed the silhouette of the struggling creature, skewered on the tip. Valle, a vast black bulk, rose from the ground, and his knife was a flicker of lightning that quenched itself in the beast's throat.

Seleva gagged as the stench of hot blood filled the clean mountain air. But she forced herself to rise as if her bones were not near to cracking with weariness. By the time the three outlaws had cleaned their weapons and straightened themselves again for walking, she was waiting for them, as if eager to go on.

She understood that they expected her to be a drag on them, impeding their speed. She did not intend for it to happen, no matter if she died there in the foothills, attempting to match her steps to theirs. As the dawn filled the sky, which was now more visible than it had been in the thicker woods below, she could see grudging respect on their weathered faces.

It amused her. They thought they were great villains, she felt certain. Two were outlaws, guilty of nothing more hideous than stealing sheep or cattle, or perhaps of killing a rival for a farm wench's favors. Strindberg was a different sort, but what that might be she had not decided. They would all blanch, she knew, if they understood some of the many terrible things she had done in order to secure Granary for her compatriots. Although she could not be called a villain, she had been forced to do villainous things, finding no alternative for safeguarding her world.

Those kidnapped negotiators had been only the beginning of her misdemeanors against what was considered lawful and decent behavior. She alone, of the leaders of the agricultural worlds, had troubled herself to learn the intricacies of the contract binding them to the Consortium of the United Worlds.

The other farming colonies had accepted the aid of legal advisors provided by the Traders, when that became the manner in which the crops were sold. Farmers, she knew from old experience, hated to clutter their busy minds with legalities. But she felt in her bones that to trust the Traders might be fatal to her people's freedom.

Ignoring the policies of other agricultural worlds, she had studied those contracts, knowing her adversary's lawyer was no friend of hers. Soon she realized the instrument was no more nor less than a sort of indenture, binding her world and all its people and its produce to the needs and whims of the economic and military interests of the Consortium of Traders.

The negotiators seemed decent and friendly, but the records she had called up over the Information Network showed her they were hatchet men, sent to guide the local governments into forms and systems that would be most easily manipulated and controlled by their masters, as well as into contracts that would hold them fast, once they realized their error. These were documents aimed at creating a state of permanent servitude among all the agricultural worlds.

She invited them to a banquet at her official home. There she drugged them, had them carried to one of her family's farms, and held them, along with all their trade secrets, hostage to the agreement of their principals to sign new and far more generous contracts. There they stayed until the Consortium consented to her terms.

The fact that her life was forfeit, if she ever left the security of her home world, did not trouble her at all. She had enough to do, and more, with putting into order the planet that now for the first time could manage its own affairs without outside interference.

She chuckled quietly, as Valle held out a hand to help her clamber over a particularly large boulder that thrust from the steep hillside.

"And what would seem funny, on a cold morning on your way to a harebrained scheme that'll surely kill you and most of those others?" grumbled Strindberg, behind them.

"I was thinking of the first man I ever killed with my own hands," she said, her tone perfectly calm. "I had many killed, of course, at my order. There were those, back in the old days, who wanted to sell out to the Traders and the Consortium in return for equipment that we could not make for ourselves and technologies that would cause us to depend totally upon other worlds. They had to go, and we couldn't afford fares off planet. So they died.

"But that was not like killing. Not really. I didn't see it done. I only saw the space where they had been, afterward. No, the first was an assassin, sent, quite justly, by the family of one of my victims." She almost chuckled at the shock registered by the tension of the brawny shoulders silhouetted against the sky ahead of her.

"He bribed his way, I suppose, into my quarters at the Stronghold. When I came in, hot and weary from my day of work, dropping my clothing on my way to the bath, he rose from behind a screen of flowering plants about the bath pool." She felt a grin quirk her cheek. "He did not expect a small woman, no matter how able, to defend herself against his great bulk and his sharp blade. I tripped him as he came, flipped over his back, and broke his neck with a choplock, before he understood that I was not still standing there, waiting for his thrust.

"I knew him, as it turned out. Not well, but I did know him." She could still feel the shock with which that recognition had registered in her mind. She sighed and stepped out at a brisk pace. The men slowed momentarily, staring at her, their eyes unbelieving.

She turned her head to smile at Strindberg. "Do not think, even now, that you might come out of a battle with me unscathed. You may know tricks that let you defeat others with some ease, but my life has been in my own hands for many years. I have invented feints and techniques that allow me to use what little size I have to its best advantage. Even now, I am far more dangerous than you would think."

Carrick grunted, and she detected a skeptical note in his gruff voice. She hoped she would not be forced, ever, to demonstrate her ability. She would die, of course, but so might Carrick. She would, if not taken unaware, leave him a cripple as she died.

* * * * * * *

The morning went swiftly, as they moved rapidly over the rough countryside. They went up into the foothills, keeping to the thickest of the forest, for now they could hear the humming from the sky that told them the Commander's airborne troops were aloft.

Seleva hoped General Coville had all his people under cover of Coldfellow Wood, for Stormwall was little more, she hoped, than a pile of smoking ruins. Even then, they would have to move fast into the hills, or those who hunted them might catch them before they reached areas too difficult for the flying machines to risk. The mountains bred dangerous air currents.

SHOCK TREATMENT, BY ARDATH MAYHAR * 73

The tracks they followed twisted around the hills, tunneling through thick stands of saplings or under the outspread branches of older trees, which shut off the sky. The sun rose higher, and Seleva felt her knees beginning to buckle slightly with every step, but she clenched her teeth and kept on.

By noon, the conical shape of Phantom Hill stood sharply against the sky, the first outlier of the ranked mountains behind it. Strindberg paused at the edge of a grassy glade that edged the stream between the last hill they had descended and the roots of the steep before them. Without speaking, he reached and lifted Seleva onto his back.

"Hold on. We've got some fancy footwork to do, and I wouldn't trust anybody who hasn't done it before to get through without falling. If we cross that clearing, anyone in the air, even out of our sight here, might spot us. We're about to do some rock climbing."

She locked her hands under his chin and her legs around his waist. The three men darted downstream to a fallen boulder, which halfway spanned the water. Beyond was a tumble of stone, shattered from some ancient slip down the side of the height. They went up it like monkeys, leaping from overgrown ledge to undercut boulder, staying always beneath a thin screen of branches, which were still laden with dying leaves. Young trees had thrust their way up between the stones, stabilizing the slide and hiding that uneasy path.

They reached the top much faster than Seleva would have dreamed, and without falling or dropping her. When they were just beneath the crest, where a cap of weathered rock protected the sharp summit, Strindberg stopped.

He let Seleva down and stared at her. "You have a signal?" he asked. "I've no great ambition to be killed by your friends, if they are already here."

She chuckled, putting her first two fingers to her mouth and sending a shrill whistle into the air. It skreed among the distant bluffs, echoing around and around like the call of a carrion bird. And in a moment there came a reply from the top of the hill.

Seleva turned to look up at Strindberg. "Lemmon is there," she said. "I will do the rest. Go back and protect your own, if you can. Help Coville, if possible. We are all in this basket together, my friend, like it or dislike it." Without waiting for his reply, she turned to climb the last rough slope, seeing Lemmon emerge into view under the caprock. When she reached the woman's side, she looked down the side of Phantom Hill, and there was no trace that any others had ever stood there beside her.

* * * * * * *

A half day and a night of rest, added to the ration Lemmon had prepared, did wonders for Seleva's energy. The troopmistress had come alone, far ahead of the rest of the refugees from Stormwall.

"Coville is going to settle the wounded and a good muster of troops, with the pregnant women and the children, in the mountains. The map you made of the old rebel hideout in the high valley was valuable for that. Then he is going to send men down into Ellanish and give the Commander's garrisons there something to think about.

"We have had spies among the troops there for months, since the danger became apparent. He wants us to go ahead of him, fast and quiet, to burn food supplies, rally the farmers, free what conscripts and slaves we can manage to, and otherwise disrupt things until he can get there."

"Alone?" asked the old woman, her silver eyes bright as coins.

Lemmon chuckled. "Even the pair of us might not be equal to all of that. No, he has groups already on the move. We will add our efforts to theirs. And then we shall see how much pressure the Commander can maintain against Tellich, when his troops are being savaged beyond the mountains."

"Intelligent," mused Seleva. "I must admit that Coville has more deviousness than I suspected at first. So we will go down the hill, up the mountains, and over as fast as possible. I know a house, not far from the edge of the farming lands, where someone I used to know lived. It is possible it may be empty. I heard that its owner died after it was commandeered for one of Theron's cronies. Winter is on its way, and we will need shelter."

She kept reminding herself of those last words as the pair of them struggled over the range, which was already swept by cold winds and the first stinging snows of the high country. She had to give herself a jolt of pain, from time to time, just to keep her adrenals working to a sufficient level to overcome her weariness and aching bones.

At last they came down the eastern slope, just before twilight. Spread below them were the neat farms and the thick woods separating each community of this Grange of agriculturists. Now that she was so near, the old woman found herself able to move more swiftly, and she led the way around an outlying complex of fields, at the farther edge of which they could see the huge storage sheds holding the harvested crops.

Even as they slid through the forest toward her goal, a flare of red light rose behind them and told Seleva that the General's commandos had fired the stores they had seen. "Efficient people, those," she said over her shoulder to her companion.

"Very. I trained them myself," came the reply. "Standish's forces will face a hungry winter, if things go well for us."

Then they were winding through the wood, Seleva's sure sense of direction guiding them toward the house that was her goal. They reached it unerringly, finding it cold and dark. Lemmon picked the lock easily, letting them into the big, faintly musty-smelling rooms.

Seleva shook away the memory of her last visit here. Darrell and Lidia had been young, their child a boy, she thought, had been a toddler. They had been awed at having the Commander of Station in their home, and she had tried hard to make them feel at ease. It had been one of her few experiences of the life of a normal family in a home without guards and weaponry. She sighed.

A bit of fire and some hot food helped the older woman recover from her efforts. When they had rested and she'd regained some of her energy, they chose a bedroom, sharing its huge bed, whose linens might smell like dust and mildew but felt totally luxurious to her old bones.

Far in the night, Lemmon stiffened to attention, waking Seleva from a fitful sleep. "There is someone downstairs," the woman whispered. "What do you want for me to do?"

Seleva Karmann thought hard for a moment. It might be an enemy, true, but if that someone was alone and moving so stealthily that even her own sharp ears could not hear him, he might just as easily be a possible ally. Any countryside held by Theron's troops would, of necessity, contain rebels and dissenters trying to elude his forces.

"Wait," she said softly. "Get into position beside the door, settle yourself comfortably, and wait. If this midnight walker comes to us, we will be ready."

CHAPTER THIRTEEN

UNEXPECTED ALLIANCE

Yace's heart stopped beating for an instant, and his bowels went watery with shock. His instinct had told him someone was in that room, he thought as he froze, feeling the tickle of the knife still at his throat. There came a sharp sound in the room ahead of him, and light glared from a hand-generated torch. He turned his eyes slowly in their sockets to see his captor. Not at all to his surprise, he saw that it was a square-built woman, whose hand was rock-steady on the hilt of her knife.

She was browned and weathered but still young, and he was glad he had not tried to resist her. He would, even now, be lying on the floor, his arterial blood washing around her feet, if he had. And Jon would be left alone in the forest, without anyone to call a friend.

When he looked at the one squeezing the generator handles of the torch, he was astonished, however, for she was old and frail-looking. She reminded him strongly of his single glimpse, months before, of the Commander, when Standish visited the post guarding the road through Ellanish.

Her quick eye saw the look of recognition, for the old woman nodded. "I am the Commander's grandmother and his sworn enemy. Who are you?"

Yace felt himself relax a bit. If these were the enemies of his enemies, then they might prove to be, perhaps, friends. Perhaps allies, for the time. "Yace. I escaped from the compound where the Station troops are located, and I came here because Darrell was my father's friend. There's someone..."—he almost said, "with me," but he caught himself in time—"There's someone I need to find, if I get the chance."

He had no wish to put Jon in peril, if these should be spies set here by Standish, for some obscure reason of his own. The old woman had looked as if she meant it, when she said she was the Commander's worst enemy, but Yace had learned one thing, if nothing else, since he had been jerked from his work in the fields. You could not trust anyone, no matter how persuasive he might seem. Only desperation had led him to trust Hakle, and it rather surprised him it turned out to be justified.

The knife moved away, and he swallowed hard. Even under Jarek's whip, even in the custody of the invaders' troop, he had not felt so much in danger. These two were ruthless and set on accomplishing some end he felt in his gut might well mesh smoothly with his own. If it allowed him a chance to even his score with Jarek, that would be even better. He found much of his planning for the future involved getting his hands on that abusive bastard.

"I came from the south," he said. "The troops have cleared a compound in the wood for a fort and built temporary shelters. There's a tall, thick fence built of heavy logs around everything. Not to keep anyone out, I think, for they seem to be sure they have us all under control, but to keep the slaves and the conscripts inside at night, when it's hard to watch them. I got away because I was helped by a sleeper someone had put into the troop."

He paused to watch the effect of his words on the pair.

The sound of the generator, whirring rhythmically in the older woman's hand, was all that broke the silence for a long moment. Then the younger held out her hand. "Lemmon," she said. "Troopmistress to General Coville of Tellich. This is Seleva Karmann. We intend to disrupt the Commander's supplies and troops here, in order to pull those beyond the mountains away from our own country, which has not been entirely conquered. Have you any objection?"

Yace thought for a moment. "There's nothing you can do that will make us any more miserable than we are. Already, we can see we're going to starve, this winter, no matter whether the crop is burnt or not. The troops are taking it all, and I heard the officer at the compound telling his sergeant that when we were all worn out and dead, they could bring in others from Sterne Rift, newly captured, who would last out the winter. They might even be able to plant the crops in spring."

He laughed harshly. "I learned the hard way that my welfare wasn't anything the Commander was going to lose any sleep over."

"I think you may be of use to us," said Seleva. "You are young. I suspect you have been working very hard for long enough to make you strong, without going so far that your health has suffered. We can use you, as long as you last. Don't be deceived into thinking that will be for long, however. The troops here are becoming seasoned, and they are dangerous. This is not going to be easy." Her eyes glinted brightest silver in the backwash of light from the torch.

Yace felt a touch of his old desperation. There had been nothing but pain and labor and danger and death since the day he had been taken from the fields to serve the Station troops. He had seen stronger men than he, older and more experienced at survival, worn down to fragile skeletons, dying between one harsh task and the next. There seemed to be no place to go, nothing to do that would make his life secure.

"Why not?" He shrugged.

The knife almost darted up again, before Lemmon saw the shrug was not a threat. He nodded reassuringly to her.

"What do you want me to do?" he asked.

"Just be ready; we have not assessed the situation, as yet," said the old woman. "We only arrived this evening, with the dusk. We may want you to reconnoiter your back trail, to make certain you were not followed. We may want you to scout the troop at the compound, if you can find a way to do it without betraying yourself and us. There are many uses for a fit young man, in the business we intend to accomplish here."

She paused, a puzzled look on her lined face. "Is there someone else there outside? I felt a twinge of pain, yet not actual physical agony. A feeling of loss and sorrow and...illness. Almost...almost childlike."

"How did you do that?" Yace asked, feeling his skin crinkle into gooseflesh. "There is a child out there. Waiting for me. I didn't want to betray him until I was sure you wouldn't send him back to the perverts in the camp."

"Ah." That was all she said, but Seleva Karmann's eyes burned brighter still, with ferocious anger. "So my grandson is encouraging the abuse of children also? I will put it down to his account, be sure of that. Now go and bring that cold and frightened child into the house. We can, if nothing else, warm and feed him."

Yace stared at her and at Lemmon, who was lighting dusty candles, which were cobwebbed and sputtery. In the flickering light, he saw their faces more clearly. Neither looked like anyone who could support the aims of Standish, whatever their own might be. He nodded.

They were not talkative, these two, and nothing was said as he turned from the bedroom into the blackness of the farmhouse again. What strange twist of fate, he wondered, was setting his road alongside that of the Commander's grandmother?

* * * * * *

Jon lay in the growing chill of the forest, listening intently. Nothing but darkness surrounded him, broken only occasionally by the shrill chirrrk of a bird that had not yet flown south for the winter. The leaves on the floor of the wood rustled as the cold wind off the mountains swept among the trees, and the boy found himself flinching at sudden gusts, thinking his tormentors were coming after him.

Jon huddled his arms around his knees and set his back more firmly against the trunk of the tree against which Yace had put him. What was happening in that black house? Was the big fellow still alive? Would he come back, even if he might be? He seemed friendly enough, but Jon had learned distrust in a harsh school. Perhaps he had been left here to die. The way his chest felt, here in the cold and the damp, that might not take long.

Tears leaked from the corners of his eyes, but he had used up his ability to cry long before. Repeated beatings had conditioned him not to sob, even when, from time to time, one of the men who used him liked such accompaniment to his pleasure. That meant more beatings and sometimes much worse. Scars of cuts and burns marked his skinny body, mementos of cruel masters satisfying their lusts.

Something shrieked in the depth of the forest. A mouse, perhaps, or a vole. The whisper of large wings passed over the small glade in front of him, and he shivered. He knew forests, it was true, but he had never liked being there alone. Not at night. And this was not his own forest, in which he had lived as a small child. Who knew what unfamiliar predators might stalk the dark hours?

Footsteps crunched briefly, then paused. He pulled himself into an even smaller ball, knowing himself to be invisible against the dark bulk of the tree. But now there came a whisper, sharp in the darkness.

"Jon! Are you still there? Come with me...I think we have found people who may be friends."

Yace. He let out a long breath, which quivered more than he liked to note, and drew another. "Really? Not troopers?"

Now the big fellow with the strong hands was very near him. Fingers, warm and oddly gentle, touched his face briefly, went to his shoulder and patted it. "They have food, and we can build another fire," said Yace.

The boy rose, feeling his knees shake beneath him. "I can't see," he said, his voice uneven. "Lead me, Yace."

"Better than that," said the young man. "I will carry you!"

Jon found himself lifted with startling ease and placed on Yace's back. "Duck to miss the branches. I think we have found a bit of safety and maybe a ration of help," said the young man, as he slid through the forest again, toward the black shape of the house against the slightly lighter sky.

As they slipped through the forest, Jon felt himself warming against Yace. Something like comfort filled his heart for the first time in a very long while.

* * * * * * *

Using the orbiting platform's capacities as a communications satellite, Jeroboah could bounce his surveillance beams into many unexpected areas of the continent. In the old days when he was one of Seleva Karmann's trusted advisors, he had managed to plant his equipment in crucial spots that he felt might, in time, need to be monitored.

Today he was quite himself, remembering all his plots and plans, his agents in place in the Stronghold, and those whom he had helped to put into position. Standish would have gone into shock if he had suspected the extent of the infiltration of his most secure sanctuary.

With Stormwall evacuated, Jeroboah knew that other rebels moved in the mountains and through the forest east of the mountains. It was time, he thought, to make arrangements for the future. Because his memory was so faulty, he had written the plan down in many places, so it would not be lost.

CHAPTER FOURTEEN

A STRANGE AND UNEASY FEELING

The Stronghold lay silent around his office, but Theron Standish was unable to relax. Something was going amiss, out there in the fields and the mountains. Even Cozarre had failed him, for his Sniffer had found Seleva was no longer in the lands controlled by the troops of Station. Sending him out into the troubled countryside, when there was possible need for his services, if things in Station grew any more threatening, was not something he felt wise.

No, the Commander intended to put him in the central control room, with his hand convenient to the activating switch that would send all of the Stronghold up with a single blast. Stormwall was now retaken, that was one comfort. And yet it was a very small one, for not a single rebel had been captured there, and the fortress had been so damaged by charges set by those who left that extensive repairs were necessary. Even the wounded, and there must have been many after the first attack, were gone without a trace.

The airborne troops had been offloaded into the fortress, their hand lasers ready and their nerves tense, but not a lance of flame or a zinging pellet had met them as they spread out and scouted the complex.

That, in itself, was something that troubled Standish. They should not have felt secure enough to slow themselves with wounded and women and infants. The ragtag militia defending the fortress should have run, panic-stricken, for the mountains. But what faint traces could be read told his officers they had withdrawn in good order into Coldfellow Wood.

That nest of vermin! He still steamed with frustration and fury when he remembered that herb woman, Lilias had been her name, who had spurned him and disappeared into the trackless wilderness.

His arm, long healed now, gave a twinge along the old break.

She and her spawn were probably at the root of much of his trouble, he thought. They were the sort who did not accept authority, did not believe in those wiser than themselves, and refused to submit to the proper exercise of power. He had known a few such, as he had gone through his life. Most of them he had used and broken and discarded, at last, when he found them and brought them into his Stronghold.

His grandmother would not have accepted that rejection, he thought. For all his hatred of the old woman, he could only admire her earlier career. It was a pity she had gone soft in her later years. He knew he owed much of his own ruthlessness and brilliance to the genes inherited from her, and he could only hope that age would not do to him what it had done to Seleva Karmann. She had been the idol of his adolescence. He still admitted that, even to his cousin.

That steely gaze had been enough to freeze him in his tracks, and her quiet voice, the words snipped from ice and metal, could direct him even toward goals he did not share. He wondered what it was that had turned her into a humanitarian and a democrat. She had shown little trace of such traits in her younger days!

He shook himself and sighed. She had spoiled him for stupid people, and that woman in Tellich had spoiled him for his pretty boys. Now he wanted women. Not women! One woman. Lilias Stringfellow Strindberg, as she called herself. But she had not been seen since his ill-fated trip into Tellich, and not a single one of his agents had been able to find any lead as to where she might have gone. She had to be still in the forest, leading the outlaws who sheltered there.

Standish did not like to think of his failures. His grandmother and Lilias had to be counted among those, so he keyed the console, calling up the latest troop strengths, supply requisitions, depot inventories. Campaigning in winter was going to require more food and other supplies, and the emptying of the storehouses in Ellanish was going too slowly. He must send a signal to his officer in charge of the occupation. Things must be speeded up, before the early snows halted everything.

He stared at the report from Stormwall. He had lost too many men, too much equipment there. The supply of carriers was limited, since the Traders declined to give him more, even in return for the rare items that were grown nowhere but on Granary. Sugarberries, dry-frozen and honeyed with the native sweetener. Blue melons. Fillet of river mammal. None of those had tempted them in the least.

Even worse was the dwindling fuel for the flame-throwing

weapons. The lasers were simple to operate and maintain, but the chemicals used in the man-burners were not found in sufficient quantities on Granary to make mining feasible. When his last reserves of those fuels were gone, there would be no more. He cursed the Traders often for their misplaced scruples.

But if his grandmother had not altered the contracts—no, he would not think of that. He refused to owe her anything, though he knew that on another agricultural world than this the Traders would have descended like locusts, once he began his work of consolidation. Long before now, they would have stripped it bare, leaving its colonists helpless, without markets for their produce or sources of manufactured goods. But they should sell him armaments!

There was a quiet tap at his door. He scanned the monitor, wondering for the thousandth time if the image there might not be that of Jeroboah. But it looked like the old woman who stayed awake late to prepare his midnight meal. Lined and bent, she stood there in the corridor, holding the covered tray, and she was so patient and uncomplaining that he was tempted to smash her flat, when he let her into the room.

He hated gray and submissive women! After Lilias they and all others seemed stale and flavorless.

He thumbed the control that opened the door, and she came into the room, her step silent, though her hip hitched as if with an old injury. She never raised her gaze to meet his...he realized he had never seen her eyes.

He gestured toward the tabouret near the console. "Put it there. And get out!"

Then he stopped her with another wave of his hand. "Look into my face, old woman. I will not have people about me into whose eyes I cannot look."

The withered features turned up toward him, and the faded eyes stared into his own. Something...faint and far away...almost was recognizable. A flash, but surely not. There was nothing in that crone to blaze up into a flash of any sort. The face was still and remote, caught, he thought, in another time and place, barely cognizant of the present.

He snorted with disgust and waved her out. When he lifted the cover, a fragrant steam rose to meet his nostrils, and he nodded. If she were not so good a cook, he would long ago have had her killed. But you did not waste a good cook, no matter how irritating her person might be.

He tasted the soup. Perfect. The bread almost rose from the plate, it was so light and flaky. The meat was tender, yet red in the middle, just as he liked it. No, she could live a while longer. If only he could dispose of his grandmother as easily as he could this aged hag! He ate greedily, forgetting the flash of the familiar in the eyes.

* * * * * * *

They might not have seemed so faded, without the drops the woman used. Her face was lined with marks that were not the tracks of time. The defiance that had almost escaped would have forced him to recognize Lilias, no matter what elaborate makeup she might use to conceal her age and true appearance. As she moved silently down the corridor, the woman was almost smiling.

She was in position. Her husband was with her, working as an undergardener. Long ago, they had been in contact with the ancient Jeroboah, and he had proposed to them a plot that would find good use for them, when it came to fruition.

When the time came to settle Theron Standish, her son would send word to her, and then she would know what to do.

* * * * * * *

But behind her in the Commander's rooms, Standish had forgotten her. Coldfellow Wood was dry now. The green sap had subsided, and the leaves were dead. The snows had not yet blanketed the forest. Coldfellow Wood could be burnt in such weather. That would rout those mavericks who hid there, as well as any rebels who might still skulk in its shelter.

And if Lilias burned with the forest? He shrugged, turned to touch the communications key. Then he stopped. If she burned...no, he could not yet face that possibility. If she died without submitting her will to his, he would be forever lessened.

Let the forest stand for a while longer. He had a war to conduct.

CHAPTER FIFTEEN

THE STRINDBERG MANEUVER

It was a strange feeling to help outsiders, Arvid thought, as the last of the refugees from Stormwall disappeared up the forested slopes leading into the harsh and almost inaccessible mountains. Those he had guided in the quickest ways toward their goal might make that hellish climb, but burdened as they were with their wounded and their young ones, he doubted it.

He approved of Coville's plans for harrying Standish's troops over the mountains in Ellanish, but he did not volunteer himself or his people to aid in it. He did not know Ellanish. He did know every inch of Tellich, from the barrens beyond Stormwall to the tops of the mountains, from the sea on the west to the border of Station.

The world of Granary seemed to be rising against the Commander at last, and he intended to use his limited strengths and his special knowledge in the best way he could find. Those troops now on Stormwall thought their war ended. They were to hold that stronghold, he felt certain, controlling the lands beneath the escarpment while Standish concentrated on subduing Ellanish and Sterne Rift, east of the mountains.

Yet he was sure that most of all, Standish wanted the wheat lands lying between the mountain chain on the north and east and the sea on the west. The troops on Stormwall could be the key to the wheat fields. He did not intend for them to have an easy task of it, even though they remained in the remnant of the old fortress.

There were ways onto the escarpment that nobody knew but those he led, and he intended to make full use of them all, before he was done. He had not hinted to Coville what he might do, and he said nothing to anyone not directly concerned in his plan. When the time came, he simply called for those best suited to help him, and led them away from the camp.

Now he slid through the wood, his back bent beneath a heavy pack. Behind him came Carrick and Garet. Their present mission was one best served by few, and the three of them were the quietest of the entire population of Coldfellow Wood. They could go unseen and unheard, when it was necessary. This first sortie against the occupation troops was the most important, for it must set the pattern for those that would follow.

They were almost at the edge where the wood thinned at the border of the goat pastures. The most easily concealed approach would be that curving to meet the eastern end of Stormwall itself, but that was the direction from which Coville's people had come when they demolished Standish's attackers. They would be watching that way closely.

Who, they would think, could slip across grassy fields, clearly to be seen by any looker by day or detected by heat seekers by night, to approach by way of the rough country at the foot of the escarpment? But there were ways, and Strindberg grinned into the twilight as he paused to allow his followers to catch up to him.

"The light is right," he said. "When it grows really dark, they turn strong lights down and play them across the grasslands and the broken country beyond. But just at twilight, they still think they can see, even though they cannot."

Garet heaved his pack onto the ground and began taking out rough cloaks, which seemed to be woven of twigs and grass and dried stuff that was the very color of the grass itself. It was amazing what determined people could create when they had need of it. Each of the men wrapped himself in the folds of one of the cloaks, covering their heads with loose hoods. The wind was cold, and the added layer was a comfort, as well as camouflage. Then they stepped out of the covering fringe of scrub trees, their backs bent enough to keep their shapes from seeming human, and began moving among the random groups of goats, which were still nibbling at the frost-killed grass and bushes.

At a ground-eating walk, they moved over the pastures toward the tumbles of stone and the crannies caused by ages of freezing winters and blazing summers. Once they reached the rough, no matter how many lights were turned toward them, they could move unseen toward their goal. The heatseekers would be hard put to distinguish them from the clusters of goats that habitually sheltered among the boulders.

The light thinned away, and darkness rolled over the grasslands. Then the halogen lights blazed into life on the height and began their rhythmic sweeps across the countryside below. Arvid chuckled, as he lay flat to allow a beam to move over him. Did those by-the-book military men think the only way to go about harrying Stormwall was by their own means? The beam passed, and the three rose and pelted forward, enabled by the darkness to make better time. The very lights they used blinded those above, no matter what sort of sensitive glasses they might use to detect intruders in the pastures.

The goats about them, untended by their absent herders and at large in their grazing land, moved irritably, baaing in low voices. That had to confuse any image the men in charge of the instruments above might receive.

Fifteen face-downs later, Arvid felt rubble instead of grass beneath his hands. Pulling his cloak tightly about him, he rolled into a ditch between house-sized stones that had fallen, ages before, from the cliffs of Stormwall. From this point onward, he and his fellows would travel fast, hidden from those on the height. When they found themselves again in darkness after disturbing a number of disgruntled goats, which had bedded down out of the wind, Strindberg felt about the boulders to his right. Here was the point toward which he had been moving.

He had hidden in this tangle of badlands from those who searched for him, long years before, leading them astray from the wood and his family and companions. He had learned every way through the maze of fallen rock, and now his fingers touched a gash, seemingly natural, that he had cut there for the guidance of those in need.

He did not speak. Coville had told him of the sophisticated listening devices carried by the Commander's military. Those could pick up speech, even a whisper, at a distance of hundreds of meters. That had been valuable information, for he had never dreamed anyone could eavesdrop on others from a great distance. All his people had been warned, and now he guided his followers by touch, using a system of taps and strokes they had devised for such use.

From time to time the stone above was washed with light as the halogens' rays swept over, but the men were concealed and used the bit of illumination to find their way even faster. Even so, it required hours to reach the area directly beneath the crannied steep of Stormwall. Once there, Strindberg found himself skirting the burnt-out hulk of the carrier that had gone over the edge weeks before when Coville and his people attacked. He had heard the tale from those he guided into the mountains, and now that he saw the evidence, revealed in the backwash from the beams overhead, he understood just how terrible that ascent had been.

Bodies, uncorrupted because of the cold weather, still lay sprawled over boulders or fallen stiffly into crevices, the burned flesh black where the carrion-eaters had not gnawed it away to gray rawness. Even in the chill, the smell was gut-wrenching.

Instead of climbing, as Falville and his people had done, Strindberg turned back east, following the foot of the cliff, remaining close under the concealing ledges and outcroppings of stone. With the help of the halogens, the area was lit enough to see, yet dim enough to conceal his people when they must dash from one overhang to the next. At last the trio reached the spot Arvid had chosen for this first foray.

There was a dark hole leading straight into the cliff. Barely wide enough to allow Arvid's wide shoulders to pass, it was smooth—almost polished—and he was able to slide along almost without effort. Behind him he could hear Garet breathing heavily, and he recalled that his large lieutenant hated being cramped into any small space. Carrick, farther back, was grunting softly as he pulled himself along.

They went so for what seemed hours, but was far less time. Then Arvid felt the change in the air pressure that told him the shaft was ahead, and he reached backward with a toe until Garet touched his foot. Three taps told him to be alert for a change. Strindberg knew he would pass that "word" back to Carrick, so he went on alone until he felt the flow of cold air from above.

He stood slowly, feeling above his head as the opening slanted upward. At last he was upright in the center of the space, feeling the air flowing downward along his body, then away through the flue up which they had come. In a few moments, his companions joined him, and he put out a hand to each in the pitch darkness.

He took Garet's hand and moved it to their right to touch the wall, polished with what must have been millennia of snow runoff from the top of the cliff. There were handholds there. He knew that well, for he had cut them himself, against future need, when he had been trapped here hiding. They led out the top, into a chasm just below the overhanging wall of the fortress.

Garet said nothing. He stretched upward, and then he was gone, climbing the slightly slanting shaft. Once Carrick was shown the rude ladder, he went too, and Arvid came behind, wondering if anyone could hear spoken words through so much thickness of stone. He decided not to risk it. The shaft itself might carry sounds to ears that he wanted to avoid.

The end of the shaft was broad, flattened so they had to crouch, and horizontal, allowing them to look out over a broken countryside that was shades of black and dark gray. The distance downward could not be seen, and Arvid thought that might be a very good thing. His fellows would not be able to see the desperate drop below, as they made their perilous way along the ledge that slanted up to meet the point where the fortress wall met the solid rock.

"Follow me," he signaled by taps on wrists. "I know the way."

And he did, though only from observing it from below, committing every outcrop, every jutting foothold, every rock and bulge and niche to memory. Now he had to pull those recollections out of his mind from beneath the accumulations of years, and trust his life to what he remembered. He put out a hand, and the groin of stone was beneath his fingers, the wind-worn hole just right for giving good purchase.

He sighed and decided to allow his reflexes to carry him through. He had absorbed all of those matters into his very fibers, at a time when his life might depend on his knowledge. And now it did.

Miraculously, nothing major had changed. No necessary handhold had surrendered to time and weather and tumbled into the chasm. No foothold had worn too shallow to accommodate his seeking toe. He arrived at the angle of wall and cliff weary, arms aching from compensating for the bruising weight of the pack still on his back, but in one piece. Once he was settled above, the others came up easily, and the three of them found themselves beside the short wall protecting the Offal Gate of the old fortress.

Seleva had told her erstwhile captor of that useful entryway, and now Arvid blessed her foresightedness. This was a way none without local knowledge would ever think might exist. The panels, the old woman had told him, were invisible from inside and outside, the chain of the counterweight so high in the gloom that only one who knew where to look could ever find it, and then, without knowledge, he would have no notion what to do with it.

They slipped around the wall to the spot measured off as Arvid moved. It must be here. The stone the old woman had described was three down, two over, with finger-holds concealed in the mortar. He slid his fingers around stones, feeling for the right spot. And, after three fruitless attempts, he found the correct block, the slot in the mortar, the finger-holds deep inside and behind a slanting cut.

He exhaled softly. Garet and Carrick leaned forward; he could feel their breath warm in the cold air, as he tugged the stone toward himself, his fingers chilled almost to numbness. And the stone moved, silent and efficient, on the greased track set in place long before by those with good reason to need a silent and secret way of disposing of inconvenient people, both living and dead.

* * * * * * *

After that, it was almost too easy. The three moved into the vast cellarage of the fortress, where shelves of ancient and unusable supplies loomed all about them. Here they used their hand-generated torches, for they could risk no stumble into clattering stacks of rusted weapons or landslide of boxes as they negotiated the basement's depths.

Once they were up the stone stairway that ended in the silent kitchens, Arvid realized those of the complement stationed in the fortress who were not asleep were on watch along the top of the escarpment. They were not risking another successful attack, no matter how secure they might feel in the partially reconstructed bastion.

The wide doorway that let onto the walled courtyard was closed against the night and the cold, but it was not secured. Arvid could see the scars of the recent battle in the thick panels of overlaid wood and metal. The door had been all but rebuilt entirely.

Those outside could come in to warm themselves and to get hot soup and bread from the braziers left filled with coals in the corridor just inside it. That was good thinking, making for alert sentries. It also was convenient for his own purposes.

Almost whistling between his teeth, Arvid shrugged out of his pack straps and let the heavy bundle down onto the flagged floor. Carefully, he unwrapped the components of the explosive charges Coville had given him for his efforts against those troops left in Tellich. Garet took pressure caps from Carrick's pack, where they had been individually packed. He unwrapped them cautiously and set them, one by one, into Carrick's hand.

Arvid and Garet strung a line of sausage-like charges along the bottom of the door, after Carrick slipped four pressure caps, spaced evenly, between the bottom of the heavy portal and the stone lintel. The adhesive they used would hold them in place as the door swung outward. And when it came back to touch the lintel, they would, Arvid hoped devoutly, blow out the front wall of the fortress, as well as removing a number of the complement of Stormwall from active duty.

Arvid stepped back and inspected their handiwork in the light of the watch-beam left in the corridor. Nothing showed. They bundled their packs together, checked for any betraying sign of their presence, and hurried back to their point of entry. That took some time, and before they were all out of the Offal Gate there came a dull boom from above, shaking down dust that had not been disturbed for centuries.

They closed the stone hastily and moved along the wall, not toward the shaft, but toward the narrow ledge leading around to the westward extension of the ridge. Above them, they could hear the clanging of gongs, the shouts of startled men, the furor of a disturbed garrison that had thought itself safe.

Surely anyone manning the listening device would be distracted.

Arvid leaned close to Garet and whispered, "There is much of the night left to us to use. And there is damage yet to be done. If we become separated, head for the shaft again and hide at its bottom. But for now, we will go and see what mischief we can find to do."

He knew of crannies worn into the stone walls by the weather, just right for holding charges that could be activated from afar with Coville's jury-rigged electrical transmitters. His companions were also inventive men. They would make themselves felt in still other ways, before the night was done.

Chuckling silently, the trio made off into the blackness, while the fortress above their heads hummed like a beehive into which a small boy has flung a stone.

CHAPTER SIXTEEN

DURK

Durk muffled a groan, as he shifted his position slightly. The ribs had almost healed, but the bruises were still sore. The less severe beating of the night before had made them worse than ever.

"Shhh!" That was Nurse Sari, making her rounds of the abandoned potato shed that served as the hospital for Station troops who had run afoul of the Commander's noncoms. "He is outside, talking with the Lieutenant. You make a sound, and he will come and beat you still again, Durk. This time, those ribs are going to break even more easily, and a splinter through the lung would finish you."

"I would as soon," the young man said, feeling his breath as a stab in his chest. "This is no life for anyone. Death is better." But he found himself watching her slender shape as she moved toward his bed. She was, he thought, not much older than he.

She bent over him, her face patched with yellow from the flickering candle she had set on the table. "Tell me you need to go to the latrine," she whispered, almost inaudibly. The look on her face made him nod.

"Need to go, Nurse!" he said urgently. "While you're here. The orderly lets me pee the bed and then lie in it."

She smiled. "Of course." Her voice was cool and professional, a total contrast to her expression. "Here, let me get you under the shoulder. That's right." She led him haltingly out of the long narrow room and into the palisaded runway that enclosed the path to the latrine.

They could hear the voices of the sergeant and the lieutenant beyond the wooden stakes, but they were hidden from view. And once inside the crude walls of the facility, they were too distant to be overheard, if they whispered.

"They are going to kill you, Durk," Sari said. "Gottenrod is a killer, not fit to be in charge of anyone, much less the sick and injured. He has you in his sights. I saw him take a dislike to another conscript once. He beat her to a pulp and left her in her blood for me to find the next morning. He hates everyone—man, woman, and child.

"They tell me he was close to the Commander once, his lover, strange as that seems, before Standish began preferring women again. He has never got over his bitterness at being set aside, and others take the brunt of his anger."

"Fine," Durk breathed. "So I'm a dead man. Knowing ahead of time doesn't seem to make me any happier."

"I intend to get you out. Sometimes, there is someone still strong enough to do something against this entire system, if he gets away, and I have smuggled a few out, in my time. They will catch me in the end, of course, and then I can only hope I die quickly. This time, I will save you. You are a good man, and I like you. But you have to do just what I say, instantly, when I show you what I need." Her head was cocked, listening for anyone approaching, but her gaze was fixed on his face.

He had not expected to feel this surge of warmth in his heart again, or to find a person who cared for him. Even if he died tonight, he knew this comfort would go with him.

Durk fastened his trousers and turned from the opening down which he had urinated. His joints were puddles of agony, his bones long shafts of pain, but in general he knew he was sound, if given time to heal completely. Shaking the stench of the latrine from his senses, he accepted Sari's arm again, and they made their painful way up the path.

Once he was lying flat on the dirty grain bags that formed his bed clothing, he stared up at her. She nodded, coolly. "You'll do now. Good night."

That left him with his thoughts, for no light was supplied in the shed for the sick. The orderly never entered it from dusk to dawn, and those who died must wait for Sari to return before they were straightened for stacking and taken away. He wondered what had brought such a kind girl into the service of Standish's military medics.

What, as far as that went, had brought him to Station? he wondered. He hadn't more than half believed the promises Standish's recruiters made to potential recruits. But he had been foolish enough to sign up, making him even more of an idiot than the conscripts, who had no choice. He was going to make his fortune, here, rise from the ranks, become Somebody, he had been certain.

His father's warnings and Yace's cautionings hadn't penetrated his thick skull. The sameness of the life on his father's farm, the labor in the fields, the familiar faces that never seemed to change, had worn upon him until he craved change, if only for the worse. He had not dreamed, in that safe and sheltered life, how much worse that could be.

He would have laughed, if that had not been so painful. So he went blithely into barracks, with his handful of personal possessions and his stout farmer's clothing, only to be stripped of everything by the men there before him. Once they were sure he had nothing else to be taken, they beat him, naked, until he blacked out.

He had thought, at the time, that no beating could be worse. Now he knew better, but then he had been very young and naive. When he woke, still on the floor amid his own blood and lying on a couple of his own teeth, the sergeant had thrown him into the showers, the supply crew had given him a sleazy set of uniforms, and a bored barber had shaved the symbol of Company T into the top of his head, thus preventing runaways from going unrecognized. A pale, shaven scalp was as good as a death sentence in Station now.

He'd thought that was the initiation, but it had proved to be only the first installment. That night, after working all day in the Shuttle port, carrying goods into the warehouses, loading foodstuffs onto the craft, he had gone into the barracks to find the entire group waiting. Now came the really tough part.

He still tasted the oily dust of the floor, the remnants of dung and straw and grit that heavy boots had tracked in from the various duties of the men living there. In addition, there was the bitter salt tang of the blood that he had spilled from his own body the evening before. They'd made him lick the floor for twenty feet on each side of his bunk, before they would let him go to the showers and wash his mouth free of the filth and his body of sweat and dust.

That had been his induction into the Great Civilizing Army of Station, the Commander's pride and the instrument with which he intended to subdue all of Granary that would not willingly surrender to his will. If there had been any God still worshipped by his people, Durk would have called on Him to curse Standish. As it was, he spared the energy for a set of silent curses of his own.

He turned on his cot and spat onto the dirt floor of the shed. The taste would never leave him, no matter how long or short his life might be. Those nights would live inside him, cankering, festering, growing more bitter and dangerous with time. If he lived, which grew more doubtful every moment, he would get revenge for that grim initiation.

Even the news, long delayed and garbled, that his father had been thrown off his land and had died of it, had not added much to his already ample store of hatred for those who helped Standish and his plots. But it must have made the slight difference in his attitude that brought him to the attention of Gottenrod, for from that time onward he had been under the eye of the noncom.

He sighed and turned again. Beyond him, in the darkness, he heard a harsh gurgle, followed by a long exhalation. Another one gone. That left fifteen in the shed. Six had died over the past three days; this was a deathtrap, without a doubt. He wondered what Sari could do. He hoped she would hurry. He hoped, suddenly and desperately, that she would never be caught at her work of saving those who could be salvaged.

When the nurse came on duty again, she tended the dead first of all. There were three by that time, and she wrote the names neatly onto her tally and noted the deaths on the charts that no doctor ever examined. Then she turned toward Durk and nodded. He looked at the corpse on the cot before her. She twitched an irritated eyebrow, and he got the idea at last. He had to die. Convincingly.

He ought to know how to do that, by this time! He had watched and listened to enough deaths, over his time as a soldier, to give him all he needed to know. Durk stiffened, arching his back slightly. A gargle of sound came from his mouth, and Sari hurried to bend over him. His death rattle was a work of art.

As she straightened, she had just the right combination of sadness and composure in her expression to satisfy the most exacting critic. The stench of the hut was such that nobody would miss that of his own released bowels.

"Another one?" asked the man with two broken arms.

"Yes," she sighed. "Four in one twenty-four-hour space. That is the record, so far. This place is an abomination, and the Consortium of Worlds should know about it. But there's just no way." She sighed again, writing her notes, listing him among the dead.

It was the hardest thing he had ever tried, lying deathly still, keeping his breaths too shallow to move his chest. His nose began to itch. He needed to shift his position desperately. But he held himself still, silent, feeling the rough and stinking cloth over his face as a welcome shield against too close a survey.

The rattle of the cart that carried out the corpses sounded in the narrow corridor between the bunks. "This one first," said Sari. "Then you can move back toward the door more easily, picking them up as you go."

He blessed her quick wits. The real corpses would be piled on top of him; he had seen the ragtags who formed the burial details work before. They noticed nothing, cared for nothing but their daily ration of raw alcohol. Even if he sneezed, they probably wouldn't take note of it. But he didn't intend to. He let them flop him onto the cart, and he remembered to hold his eyes open in a deathlike stare, as they shoved the covering back onto the bed, to be used (without washing) for the next comer.

It wasn't easy to stay motionless, to keep from focusing his gaze, to hold his face still, but he managed to do it until the next body flopped onto him. Then, partially hidden, he relaxed a fraction of his tension. Maybe there was, indeed, a chance for him to live.

Once the pile of bodies was rolled outside, Sari presented her list to the sergeant for his approval, before sending them to the composting beds. Durk listened, his skin almost as cold as that of the corpse directly above him, as Gottenrod read the list.

"That recruit Durk's gone?" The tone was suspicious, and the ugly face was screwed into a grim mask.

"He hemorrhaged in the latrine yesterday," said the nurse. "I wasn't at all surprised. There must have been internal bleeding for a long time."

"Pellot, Darstang, Benoit, too. Thinning out, aren't they?" His tone was filled with satisfaction.

There was the sound of scribbling on paper, and the cart began moving again. It was pushed through the hidden gate in the wall and into the thick screen of forest that separated the compound from the fields and the stench-ridden composting area, where bodies were recycled into fertilizer.

Once it had gone around several bends in the track, Durk began moving, slowly, subtly, to clear himself of the weight holding him down. It wouldn't do to make it this far, only to be suffocated by a dead man. He managed to peer between the interlocked legs of his companions, who had been laid alternately head-to-foot, and watched the man pushing the cart. His jaw was slack, his gaze fixed on some inner vision that did not include anything his hands were doing. The others must be ahead of them, for there was no sign of them behind the pusher.

Now he could smell the composting site. The breeze brought the stench through the trees from the north, and he almost retched, thinking his own body was supposed to add its own putridity to that always growing decay. The path led them out of the wood, and the cart stopped on the brink where new refuse was dumped. The three men gathered at the small shed to get the spades and the wooden pushers with which they would deposit their load.

It was the time, or the time would never come. He heaved himself sideways, toppling one of the bodies onto the ground. So intense was his need to get away that the pain of moving didn't reach him until he was inside the fringe of forest, concealed behind a clump of sugarberry.

He didn't wait there. Those three were spaced out, but they might notice that the body had no good reason to fall off the cart. They just might even realize they had started out with four but ended up with three. But probably not. They weren't much more mentally alive than the bodies on the cart.

Every move was pure agony, but he shoved with his feet, elbowing his way into the thorny undergrowth. Punctures of many kinds added to his discomfort, and an occasional slither or hiss from deeper in the bush gave him pause, occasionally, but he kept going. Only when he couldn't move at all did he stop his efforts. He had no idea how far he had come, but the slant of the light through the trees indicated it was past mid-afternoon. He had left behind the scrub that underlay the lesser forest, and now he was lying on a smooth mat of dead leaves beneath large hardwoods.

That told him he had to be deep into the wood, for he had come through such growth on his way to join Standish's army. Only an hour of easy walking separated him from the populated center of Station. He was thirsty. The scanty food given the outcast sick in the shed had worn out a long while before. But more than anything, he was exhausted with effort and with pain. Without trying to find a more comfortable position, he let his face drop onto the leaves, and sleep claimed him.

When he woke, it was completely dark. No glint of a star showed through the dense cover of fall leaves still clinging to the trees. The second moon was tiny, its light unable to penetrate even a scanty growth of forest. The larger moon was on the other side of its lazy trip around the planet.

The wood was still, for many of the small creatures had gone into winter quarters. Birds had followed their ancient autumn flyways southward. Insects occasionally chirred from tree bark or beneath the mulch, but the night was very quiet. He found he was listening to water...a distinct chatter of shallows over rocks. His mouth suddenly drier than ever, he began to crawl painfully toward the sound.

He found the spring by splashing directly into it, his head going under for an instant, before he managed to find bottom with both hands and push up and back. Then, his body anchored firmly on the narrow mud bank edging it, he drank and drank. He had no food, but with water he could last for a long time. Long enough to heal, perhaps. Long enough to dream of going home again to the house his father had been forced to leave. Long enough to plan his revenge against the troops of Standish and the thief who had taken his family home.

He fell asleep again, this time a deep and healing slumber, but he dreamed of fire and death.

* * * * * * *

When Durk opened his eyes, he was almost unable to remember where he was and what he might be doing in so unlikely a spot. He lay in a hollow lined with dead leaves and walled with fern and moss. Not the hospital! Then he moved, and a symphony of aches, stabs, and twinges reminded him that his body was damaged badly. His head was hot, and when he tried to stand he found himself too dizzy and weak to remain upright.

His stomach rumbled, feeling entirely empty, but there was no food. He would do without, gladly.

He dropped to his knees and drank again, tasting the stone from which the spring rose, the tang of waterweed and mineral. But his head spun, and he almost fell into the basin. With some effort, he pulled himself back into the tangle of shrubs and vines and pushed himself among the leaves, trying to find some warmth. The wind was cooling, and without food in him to warm his blood, he was chilling.

He drifted away on a tide of fever. From time to time he woke enough to crawl to the water and drink, but he seldom remembered it until he found dampness on his ragged shirt. Darkness and daylight seemed to follow each other too rapidly across the sky, time after time, and he grew more and more lank, though he was too groggy to understand that. But there came a time when he woke fully, staring up through interlocked branches at the late fall sun. His mind was sharp, cleansed thoroughly by the combination of fever and fasting. He knew he must move, or he would die and leave his bones to guard the spring.

That thought forced him to push himself up onto his hands. His arms trembled with the stress of completing the move, but at last he stood, holding tightly to a pale sapling, while the world settled again into stillness.

"I have to go. Back. Home," he said aloud. "Back home." He looked down at the water despairingly. There was no way to carry any with him, and sometimes, in the autumn, the forest was dry. But he knew what he had to do, and he staggered a step to catch another tree trunk.

One tree at a time, one step at a time, Durk was going back to the house where his father and mother had lived.

CHAPTER SEVENTEEN

MAKING HOLES IN WALLS

Yace found himself amazed at the quality of his new acquaintances. Seleva, aside from being fragile-looking and old, was tough and quick, and she knew things concerning the different areas on Granary that he had never dreamed. Lemmon, on the other hand, was very quiet, always on the alert, and he knew that she was deadly. He could still feel her knife at his throat whenever he looked at her.

Both had softened in their attitudes when he brought Jon into the farmhouse. That pleased Yace, for he had formed an attachment for the boy. If his own life had been full of hard work and pain, how much worse the child's had been! His obvious illness commanded the women's concern at once, and Seleva had concocted aromatic teas for him from a supply in her pack. These seemed effective, for overnight his breathing improved and his cough began to leave him.

In the three days since their first encounter, their tiny group had begun making plans for Standish's occupying army. They had linked up, by means of Yace's long legs, with the squads that went about burning crops and making lightning attacks against groups of the enemy caught outside the walls of the compound. Yace's long familiarity with the area served them well, as he knew the best places where a guerrilla force might conceal its camps.

Much of the year's grain and root crop was now ash, and the local people were being encouraged to join Coville and his people in the high country, carrying with them all the foodstuffs they could find. Ellanish was about to become a lively battleground.

It was the compound that was a problem to the guerrilla groups. The thick log walls that surrounded it were impervious to the weapons they had to use, and the troops sheltering behind them were armed with sophisticated weapons from the manufacturing worlds. Their arsenal of anti-personnel weapons was fearsome, for Standish had bought everything from motion-activated automatic lasers to gas powered handguns modeled on the ancient Uzi.

Some of those in the rebel group had faced those armaments; from the seared burn scars and the puckered puncture wounds he could see among them, he shuddered at the thought of going up against the outpost. A frontal attack would be suicide, and they hadn't enough numbers to risk one. It was going to require intelligence, rather than firepower, to reduce the post.

On the fourth night, Seleva called a council of war. Lemmon had maps spread over the polished floor of the main room, and Yace had built up a fire of dried wood, which emitted little smoke. From round about, summoned by Jon, who made a wonderfully silent and unobtrusive messenger, four of the commando leaders came to compare notes.

Fresto was not much taller than the boy, yet he was a tough little fellow with a face that seemed carved from a hardwood root. Killek, beside him, looked like a bear, his dark furry pelt covering his chin, neck, and chest, making his cloak look redundant. Beside them, Lister seemed like a porcelain doll, out of place in such company. But her hands were rough with work, and her eyes held fires that no easy life could kindle. Those eyes glanced often at Darwood, the last of the commandos to arrive.

Yace understood her distrust. The man looked too smooth, too relaxed, too prosperous to be one of the desperate band making a stand against the troops of Station. His quick smile was too brilliant, his eyes too bright and mocking.

Yace disliked him on sight, particularly when he adopted a patronizing air toward Seleva Karmann. But the young man said nothing. He was a beginner at this sort of work, and he knew Seleva and Lemmon could handle anyone who threatened to disrupt their efforts. He was relieved when Seleva invented an errand and sent the fellow away to make contact with another group deeper in Ellanish's farmlands. That told him she, too, had felt some danger in Darwood.

"Here," Seleva said, bending over the wide map spread before the hearth. "The compound commands the intersection of the main roads, the north-south one leading down into Station and up toward Sterne Rift. There." She ran a blue-veined finger along a line on the map.

"The other road leads up into the mountains to the coal mines, across this area and back to the coast. Colyer was founded there as a port city for shipping fuel to other points around this continent. It is little used these days. Only the fact that Theron is too set in his views to value what he calls unsophisticated methods of transport saves us from even worse problems than we already have. If he had thought to ship his troops and equipment by sea, there would be little we could do about it."

Lemmon stood before the fire. Without looking at the map, she said, "Removing the command from that post would free the roads for those who will follow us into Ellanish. Going through the forest is very difficult, as we found for ourselves a few days ago. The fields are wide open to view—we know there are those in Ellanish who spy for Standish, and we must avoid their notice as much as possible. So we need to clear away that walled compound."

Killek piped up in his surprising soprano. "What about the agent inside the walls?"

Yace found himself the focus of Seleva's intent gaze. "He is a good man," he said. "But I suspect Hakle won't have a chance to do anything much. After I got away, and Jon after me, they are going to be watching everybody too closely."

"Yes," said Seleva. "Which is why I want to destroy the wall. Once there is no shelter for the Station forces, we will control Ellanish and its roads."

Fresto had been staring down at the map. Now he fixed his dark gaze on the old woman, the wrinkles around his eyes deepening. "How?" he asked.

Yace knew all the rest were wondering the same thing. But Seleva was looking at the map, her brow wrinkled with thought, her fingers crumpling the edge of the sheet of paper. "The forest has grown even thicker and taller, since I was a girl," she mused. "The rear wall...is that where you came over, Yace?"

He moved closer, found the compound on the map, and pointed to the spot in the corner where the wall of the latrine abutted the outer one. "There," he said.

"And the forest...how near does it come to the wall now?"

Yace thought back. It had been dark, but he had taken several strides before he was under cover of the trees. "I was going fast. Took...maybe four steps, and the fourth took me under the branches. Say three or four meters. Five to be on the safe side—I was moving fast."

She nodded. "And the forest is really thick beyond that cleared strip?"

Jon's voice startled them all, rising from the chimney corner where he huddled, holding his knees against his chest. "Very thick. Like a wall itself, almost. They used to let me outside, sometimes, when men go after firewood. I look about some, case I ever get the chance to run."

"Then we will destroy that wall. It is going to take a lot of work and many hands to do the task, but I know how, and now I know where. Can you get me a dozen strong people, capable of digging for about fifty yards through heavy black soil, thick with the roots of trees?" she asked Lister.

The young woman nodded decisively. "There are a dozen in my own group who will come. All are able. Most are rather small, too, which should help. But are you certain that you can bring down that wall? And what will we do when it does come down?"

"I can make a hole that Standish could ride one of his carriers through," said the Commander's grandmother. "As nearly as we can figure to the time it is going to fall, we will create a distraction on the other side of the compound, taking every available trooper there to repel the attack. Fire arrows should do the job, making a lot of excitement without depleting our stores of real explosives too much. We will have need of that later, I fear, once we are inside the post."

Seleva was not one for talking, once she had made her plan. Yace saw she did not intend to reveal the details of her thinking to anyone who might be captured and forced to talk, and he found himself approving. Each of the council was told what to do, and they left at once, slipping away into the darkness like ghosts, and leaving Yace to wonder.

But morning found him busy. It was necessary to find a way around through the forest, avoiding the road and all the major tracks connecting the now overgrown farms.

Jon had been right. The forest was almost like a series of walls, each thicker and thornier than the last. If it had not been for the boy, it would have taken Yace much longer to find a path through, cutting a way along which those to come could bring their tools and the timber Seleva demanded. As he hacked his way through a thicket of sugarberry, Yace thought of the houses that were being demolished to provide that timber. He had known most of the people who lived in them, and now they were all gone, dead or prisoners in Station. The Commander had a lot to answer for, and he only hoped this difficult expedition was going to do some good.

Jon appeared beside him. "Not far now," the boy whispered. "She said stop about ten yards from the edge of the strip. Couple more good thickets, and you be right there. I lined it up with the wall, too, just the way she said. What she going to do, Yace?"

"Plot and plan," groaned Yace. "We're the ones who will do all the work. As usual. I just hope she knows what she's doing."

Jon looked serious, in the chilly light that filtered through the interlaced branches above them. "I think she knows more than we ever will," he said, his tone sober.

Four hours later, Yace found himself hoping the boy was right. He had seldom worked so hard, even in the fields or under Jarek's whip. He and the people Lister brought had cleared a space on the floor of the wood that was about four feet wide by five long. Angling downward at a decline, strictly supervised by Seleva, they had dug through roots as big as tree trunks, networks of lesser growths, and past a layer of rock that was very hard on both picks and muscles.

Seleva whisked back and forth, peering through her glass toward the wall, which was squared up exactly with the line of their excavation. She was constantly measuring the rate of descent through the soil as well. She insisted that the tunnel be shored up solidly with the dry and weathered planks that had been parts of farmhouses and sheds and barns. So, in addition to digging, they were also building four walls of wood, braced up by eight-by-eights every six or eight feet.

The day wore out, along with the laborers. When it was too dark to see clearly, Seleva led the way back to the house and they all sank wearily to the floor before the fire, while she rummaged about and prepared a filling meal. There was no need to urge any of those who had worked on the dig to go to bed early. Fortunately, the big old house had ample rooms and huge beds, into which they piled gratefully.

Yace woke with a foot in his face. "Mmmrph!" he grumbled, as he rolled over and put his own feet on the floor. Jon's thin face popped up beside him, and Killek growled like the bear he looked, as he heaved up on the other side of the bed. "Who else is in here?" the hairy man asked.

One of the young diggers that Lister had brought dug his way out from under the covers and yawned. "Just me. Sammi. Do I smell food?"

They did, indeed, and after a huge breakfast, accompanied by the warning that they would not pause to eat again before night, the group set out again for their project.

The shaft went more easily once they were past the root layers of the smaller growths, and the rocks thinned to an occasional loose layer. The black soil was wet and heavy, but they managed to make a lot of headway before night drove them in again. And all the while, Seleva was measuring, sending Lemmon to stand with a staff on which she sighted to make certain the line of the dig did not deviate.

It took them six days to dig their shaft half of the way along the wall's length, neatly underground and invisible to any watcher. Shored all the way with dry timbers, the thing looked like a mine-shaft at its point of origin, and there was no question of any cave-in, which reassured but puzzled Yace.

From the cover of the wood, he rested and marveled at how untouched the space between the forest and the wall seemed, even though people were continually passing beneath the gray, frozen grasses. The men patrolling the top of the wall seemed to notice nothing.

On the seventh morning, Seleva sent the workers back to their groups and went, with Yace and Jon, back to the mouth of their tunnel. The floor of the forest was thick with dried leaves, and she immediately began scraping together a pile of them.

"You and the boy carry these into the shaft," she told Yace. "This will make a good hot fire, and when we add branches and deadfall, that will catch the timbers nicely."

"You mean we're going to burn it?" Yace asked, his tone full of shocked disbelief. Had they done this terrible work, just to provide an old lady with a bonfire?

"Yes. Don't argue, carry!" And she pushed a great armful of stuff into his arms and nodded toward the opening.

When the tunnel was filled to her satisfaction with debris from its mouth to its end, the old woman bent and laid a fluffy string along the raw earth of the floor, pushing its end among the brittle leaves and twigs. When that was done and she seemed satisfied with it, she struck fire from her striker and kindled a small flame in a pile of tinder. She applied that to the end of the string, and the spark began crawling along the length with terrible slowness.

"What is that going to do?" asked Yace, following her back along the path, yet turning his head to try to see smoke. But there was none—the shaft vented itself among growth too thick to show the thin haze, for the old wood, dried for generations, burned hot and almost smokelessly. No one in the compound, beyond the layers of trees and bushes, could possibly see a thing. But what good was this going to do?

"That is going to bring down the wall, right at the center where the weight is greatest," said Seleva, picking her way around a thorn bush that had fallen back into the path. "The shoring will burn out, beginning at this end and moving toward the other, getting slower as the air depletes itself. That will leave a hole beneath the great weight of the log wall.

"At the center, where the weight is greatest, the open space will not support the tons of wood on top of the thin layer of soil. And it will sink, not too quickly but with great determination, into the ground, leaving a tumbled gap through which our people can move to take over the post."

"But the troops," protested Yace. "They are better armed...."

"...and they will be fighting off an attack from the road, as well as one from behind them. Believe me, young Yace, this will work. I saw it happen at Sterne Rift, years ago when I was a beginner. This one is planned even better than that. And my opponent is a fool, which helps. Theron does not trust intelligent men as his officers."

Yace held his tongue. She might think the Commander of Station was a man ill-balanced enough to officer his troops with fools, but to normal people he seemed more of a monster who had the luck of a thousand imps.

* * * * * * *

They found Lemmon in the farmhouse, calculating times and surrounded by the preparations for the fire arrow campaign. She smiled absently, as they entered the room. "It may be going to snow," she said. "That will add its own confusion to ours, which may be to our advantage."

"Did the others report in?" asked Seleva, sinking wearily into one of the cushioned chairs. "I want to know they are all in place, when the time comes. Do your figures come out with mine? About noon in two days?"

"More or less. This is not a precision instrument, you know." Lemmon wound a strip of cloth around a shaft and dipped it into a pot of pitch. "We are going to have to be in place hours before and wait until we get a report from those waiting behind. I hope it works well; we need to remove that thorn from our sides. And once it is done, Standish is going to be so furious he may do something stupid."

Seleva sighed. "Never stupid," she said. "Theron is mad, but he is brilliant, in ways that I am not, just as my skills lie in directions he doesn't know exist."

Jon slipped up to sit beside Seleva's feet, near the fire. "I want to fight, too," he said, his tone soft and sad. "I want to hurt them."

Yace turned to his own task, checking bowstrings and flexing the old weapons for signs of rot or cracks. He didn't want to think about what the boy had said, but the quiet words rang through his mind as he readied the dusty remnants of ancient wars.

CHAPTER EIGHTEEN

A LONG WAY HOME

Durk wondered, many years afterward, what instinct sent him toward his home through the forests of Station and the foothills lying below the mountain chain. He was not rational most of the time. He was barely alive, in fact, dizzy with hunger and weak from the abuse he had suffered.

From time to time he thought of Nurse Sari. She had risked her life to send him away, alive and possibly able to fight against their mutual enemy. Her face floated before him, against a background of dead leaves and frost-touched branches, and her smile kept him going. He might go back, one day, to Station and rescue her from her bondage in the Medic service.

It got colder. Light snow sifted down through the trees, powdering the dead leaves of the forest floor and making his feet go numb. What with that and his empty belly, he felt almost disembodied, floating along like a ghost, yet always pulled, straight as a string, toward his goal.

When the voice spoke, he thought it was another delusion, like those he had been having for days. "Ho, there! Who are you? Stand or be shot!"

He laughed softly, pausing for a moment to savor the joke. A delusion was going to shoot him, or a man, if this was one, was going to shoot a ghost? Perhaps it might be for the best. He found his terrible desire to live had dissolved in the chilly air, leaving him drifting like a dead leaf toward a half-forgotten goal. Why had he wanted to go home? His father was no longer there.

Tears came to his eyes, and he fell to his knees in the thin layer of snow. A dark shape came from the interlaced branches and a fur-gloved hand reached to touch his shoulder. He shrank away. Being eaten by one of the carnivores of the forest was not his choice of a way to die.

"Here, Arvid! We've got a sick man." It was a real human voice, and the hand, now helping him to rise by clasping his arm, was no paw full of claws.

He opened his eyes and stared up though a haze that seemed a part of his eyeballs. "Who?" he croaked. "Where?"

Another fur-clad shape approached and bent over him from what seemed a great height. "Who, indeed? We are from the north and west, and that is all you need to know. But you are no enemy, I think. I see the Commander's insignia on what's left of that robe you're wearing. You're a runaway from his troops, I'll wager. We've had more than a few of those in the past months. Come with me!"

He rose and turned away, and Durk tried to call after him, to tell him he thought he couldn't walk another step. But the big fellow who had first found him lifted him as if he were an infant and carried him swiftly away through the ice-laden bushes along the path.

* * * * * * *

He woke, after a long, long time of drifting through gray-black mists, to see above him the low roof of a hide tent. For the first time in what seemed years, he was warm, though his feet were filled with jabs of lancing agony. He sighed and moved, pushing back the fur blanket that wrapped him in its folds. At once, someone came to stand beside the pile of skins on which he lay. A woman, tall and stern-looking, bent to lift him easily into the crook of her arm.

"Eat," she said, putting a horn spoon to his lips. "Broth. It will make you strong again."

He wanted to be hungry, but it had been too long...his lips and his stomach had forgotten how to work together. However, he sipped obediently from the spoon, until the woman was satisfied he had enough. Even then, when she laid him back on his bed, his belly quivered and rolled, uncertain what to do with this unexpected burden.

She knelt beside him, and beyond her he could see an open tent flap and a fragment of branch-laced sky. She wiped his face, and he realized that the small effort of swallowing had made him break into a profuse sweat. "Where am I?" he managed to ask, at last. "I was in the wood, going home. And then...I forgot why."

"You are with us," she said, with sublime confidence. "I am Nedra, and my man is Arvid, who, with Garet, brought you in. In time, he will talk with you, and we will decide what to do with you. But for now you must rest and eat and regain some strength."

Durk had never considered himself as quick-witted as Yace, who could return insults with barbed intensity or think his way out of trouble with inspired lies. But the time he had spent in Station, as well as his painful encounters with Gottenrod, had waked his lazy wits to the potential he had never troubled to use.

He turned his face up to hers. "You are, I think, fighting my enemy. The Commander. I just came from Station. It may be...when I get strong enough, it may be I can help with that." Then he winced, as pain twinged deeply. "What's wrong with my feet?" he asked.

"We had to cut off some of your toes," she said, her eyes meeting his without evasiveness. "It will hurt for a bit, but you will be able to walk, once they heal enough. You have enough left to help you balance."

She rose and turned toward the door flap, fastening it behind her. Lying in the half-light, Durk began to check over his battered body. The ribs, strangely enough, seemed to have healed somewhat, even as he struggled through the forest. His contusions were still dark, but the soreness had almost gone. Only his feet were masses of agony, and he knew that would pass with time.

He listened to the murmur of activity outside the tent in which he lay. Children spoke, though none cried or shouted playfully. Women and men talked briefly, as if passing instructions among themselves. There was none of the careless laughter or quarreling you might expect in a permanent village. This was a war camp, he was certain.

The weather had probably pinned them down here. But where had they come from? Where did they intend to go? He wondered without finding an answer, and he drifted off to sleep filled with questions.

* * * * * * *

When he woke, the huge man he had seen before was sitting on a three-legged stool beside the pallet, staring off into some distance that did not please him, for his mouth was thinned to a narrow line, and a furrow separated his bushy brows. Durk moved his legs, and the man focused on him, his gaze assessing this newcomer.

"You were a conscript?" he asked.

Durk sighed. "No. A fool—I volunteered. I thought I would go to Station and make my fortune and come home to the farm to look down on everyone I knew. Two years—it's made an old man of me, not a wealthy one. The sergeant took a dislike to me."

"Ahhh." The narrow mouth widened into a smile. "I am Arvid Strindberg. You are?"

"Durk. My father had a farm beyond the mountains, near the western edge of Ellanish. The Commander..."—he felt his voice tremble—"...seized the farm and put my father out of his home. Friends managed to send me word when he died." He bit down on the last word, holding his face still with considerable effort.

"And how did you escape? I happen to know everyone around Station is required to watch for runaways, and your hair has not grown out properly, though it looks to have had some time to regrow since it was last shaved."

Durk put up a hand and felt the rough stubble of hair on the top of his head. "I was in the sick ward. Not the hospital, the other one, where they put the ones they want to die. The nurse did it. All I had to do was to play dead."

"Sari...." Arvid's voice was thoughtful. "So she is still alive and doing her work. I had wondered if she could last so long." Again he looked someplace inside himself, as if looking into the future or the past.

"She was wonderful. It scares me to think what might happen to her, if the sergeant ever catches on to what she's doing." Durk shifted again and tried to sit.

Arvid helped him up and braced him, as they stood together in the flap of the tent, watching the early cook fires blinking into being, each small and self-contained and made of dry wood that gave little smoke.

"This isn't your permanent camp," said Durk, surveying the scene.

"We came from the forests of Tellich," said the big man. "And now we are going to war. But we must wait; there is heavy snow already in the heights, and our goal lies over the backbone of the range. There will be no moving about country in this weather, even by the troops from Station. So we wait for a chance to move safely, with all our people and their supplies."

"Against Standish," murmured Durk. "You move against the Commander...I want to go with you. I want to see the bastard lying in his blood."

"Lie back," said Strindberg. "I want to ask you how you got away, unseen, from Station. The roads, I know, are under electronic surveillance always, besides being so littered with invisible traps that without the proper keys travel along them is impossible. The fields are watched day and night. What route did you take to make your way so far, even near death as you were?"

"They put the bodies of the dead in a great compost heap near the edge of the forest. The stench is so terrible that nobody lives near, and anyone who is left to watch falls ill and dies. The gate leading into the path to it is unknown to everyone except those who carry away the dead. I was taken away through that gate. I think it was secured only with a chain and a padlock. They were going to put me into the heap, thinking I was dead, but I slid from the cart and into the bushes, and from there it was easy, except for my injuries and the fact there was no food."

"So if a group not too large made its way back along your trail, it would end at that compost heap, amid the stench of rotting bodies that will be used for fertilizer on the Commander's crops? And at that gate, leading into an all but unused portion of the enclosure of Station?" The deep voice was almost a purr.

"Yes. If I were well enough, I could lead them fairly well, though I was feverish and out of my head for much of the time. Still, I think I could find the way back."

"Hold that thought in mind. By the time the snow lets up so my people can go onward, your feet should be well enough to carry you, although painfully, back the way you have come. I want to scout this unobserved route into the heart of Station. I want to carry news of it to those who wait in the heights, counting the months of winter while they get ready to fall upon our enemies."

Durk felt a surge of warmth. There was still something he could do to avenge his father. He reached to catch the calloused hand lying near his own. "I will go with you. I will show you. But I want you to try to get Sari out alive, before anything happens to her. She is too good to let those animals destroy her."

"I agree," said the voice. "And I will, if it can be done, for she is the daughter of my uncle, and my kin."

CHAPTER NINETEEN

WAITING IS A TIRING THING

The Commander of Station was weary of waiting. Winter had come down hard on the mountains north of his country. No matter how he hounded them, troops and supplies could not move in the deep snow and the treacherous thaws that followed one another down from the north.

The most important post in Ellanish sent discouraging reports, the messengers arriving half-frozen, despite being able to ride in the enclosed carriers. Too much of the food supply he had intended to confiscate for his troops had burned in the fields or in storage, leaving his men ill-fed and discontented. Guerrillas hounded those who tried to guard the last remaining granaries. The countryside seemed to teem with rebels, intent upon preventing the successful occupation of their country. Not even automated weapons keyed to motion sensors had been able to stop the predations entirely.

He fumed at the delay, but even he could not hope to change the weather, and he fretted to no purpose. Frustration had always put him into a wicked mood. Being trapped, as he was, by his own fears as well as the weather, he knew that even his cousin was avoiding him.

His grandmother was still among the missing, and his old knowledge of her character told him she was plotting against him. Even he was no match for her in many sorts of subtlety and craft, and he shivered, at times, to think of what she might decide to do. It was unjust that she should blame him for learning by studying her own history. In her later years, she had gone soft, but he had read, as a child, the accounts of her rule over Station. That was a tale that had always made him shiver, even while feeling pride in her abilities.

She was no better than he, when it came down to the question, and she had no right to judge him now. Her recent years could not wipe out the record of blood and conniving that had tightened the grip of her family on Granary. If she had only remained the same, between them they could have reduced this world to a fiefdom, and harvested all the profits from the Traders for themselves. They would be an unbeatable combination.

He looked again at his layout of troops and projects. Those up on Stormwall were freezing to no purpose in their newly damaged fortification, for no activity had been noted in the lands below, forests and fields alike, for weeks. There was no point in invading Wheatlands, for it was buried in snow. Flying craft had examined Coldfellow Wood without detecting any trace of those who had been hiding there.

Yet if he withdrew from Stormwall those rebellious farmers might well occupy the fortress again. He could not afford another campaign like that which had conquered the place. The loss of men and equipment was impossible to recoup. Perhaps he should have the fortress razed. But he had an uneasy intuition that such an action would suit his enemies even more than it would fulfill his own purposes.

Standish sighed and turned from the table. If only the winter would ease, so he could position troops in key locations! He touched the console of his most private computer, where his personal records were kept, accessible only to him and impossible to access from the outside. Even its power source was supplied by solar-charged batteries.

He typed in the word CONQUEST, which opened his favorite files. The digital screen came to life, and words began to scroll, as he pressed the key. Invasion plans. Grandmother. Tellich. Lovers, Male. Lovers, Female. Lilias...he passed that one quickly. And even as he did, he had the fleeting thought that never had he been loved by (or loved) any human being. His grandmother, perhaps, had loved him, in her cold and distant way. His orphaned childhood had been lonelier than she liked, he was sure, but when she came to visit him in his quarters that had made him subtly uneasy.

Then he found himself staring unbelievingly at the words that came to rest in the center of the screen:

GREETINGS, THERON.
YOUR GRANDMOTHER HAS A SURPRISE
FOR YOU.
AND SO DO I!

JEROBOAH

He felt his heart cramp in his chest, and he fumbled for the vial of medicine his physician had prescribed for these nervous attacks. This had to be a delusion. There was no way in which anyone outside this room could get into that system. It was so private as to be almost nonexistent. If he forgot the code, he would not be able to access it himself!

He swallowed the drops and breathed deeply, sitting back in the comfortable chair he favored. He was too worried, too absorbed in his plans. He must rest more, as the physician had advised, particularly now that he could do nothing until the weather eased. There came a timid tap at the door.

Standish frowned. He had summoned no one. But he shrugged and said, "Come."

It was the old woman who served in the kitchens and cooked his late meals. She carried a tray, which held a steaming pot and a covered plate.

"Colonel Karmann suggested that you might need something hot, as the Stronghold has grown so chilly. The heating system has a problem, but he said to tell you it will be repaired soon."

It was the longest speech he had ever heard her make, but he listened to the frail and quavering voice impatiently. He had not noticed the growing chill of the room in his concern for other things, but now he found his feet almost numb and his fingers and nose too cool for comfort.

"Good. You may go." He watched her leave the room, and his mouth clenched with contempt. What a horrible old woman she was, gray and stooped and shriveled. Cook or no, he might have to execute her, simply to improve the look of the Stronghold.

He poured a cupful of the steaming herb tea. It smelled faintly minty, with something of apple and something of citrus in the scent. A good combination for a cold day, he thought, taking a sip. The hot liquid was spicy, aromatic, and it curled nicely into his tense belly. He relaxed and removed the napkin from the plate. Hot teacakes. His favorites.

He decided to allow the old woman to live a while longer, for they were made like those he had loved in his childhood. Only she and his detested grandmother, on the rare occasions when she coddled him, could make them just right. He nibbled a cake, sipped the tea. The message on the screen was gone, removed along with much of the file by his desperate fingers on the keys. Now the thing stared at him blandly, without menace.

Yes, he needed rest. He needed coddling, and Karmann seemed to understand that. This was just the sort of break he had required, without knowing it. When he went to work again, he would be filled with fresh energy. His eyes closed, as he stretched back in the chair. Ahhh...he felt better than he had for some time. He must rest more often.

* * * * * * *

Something clinked in the room, and he opened his eyes. For a moment the shape wavered, seeming like the old woman. Then Jeroboah stood there, grinning, in the middle of his antique carpet. As he watched in horror, the old man opened a small case in his hands and took out an injector. "I have something for you, Theron. You may not enjoy it, but it is something you need to experience. Just hold still for me...." The voice was strange and distant.

He flinched away from the injector, but he seemed paralyzed, incapable of rising and calling for his guard. The thing touched his arm and hissed softly. A deeper lethargy filled him, and he sank back into the chair and into darkness.

* * * * * * *

Feeling as if he were waking from a nightmare, Standish looked around him. Then he stiffened with horror, a shout dying away in his throat. He was no longer in his chambers, surrounded by the troops of the Stronghold. He was in a rough hut, and he lay on his back on a cot covered with stinking sack sheets and a skimpy blanket.

Around him were other cots, each with someone lying flat beneath the inadequate covering. He could hear the rattle of teeth in the icy room, and he could see his own breath freezing in the air before his face.

"Here, you mustn't move so much! You will open your stitches!" The voice was concerned, gentle but firm, and he turned his head to see a young woman wrapped in a woolen cloak, coming from a room at the end of the long dormitory. She turned his pillow and tucked the blanket around him carefully. She took a chart from the foot of his bed and made a notation, before offering him a capsule from a large jar that stood on the bedside table.

He shook his head. He didn't know where he was or what was wrong, but until he did he did not intend to take any strange medication. "Nightmare," he mumbled.

She nodded. "I can't blame you. Just don't let the sergeant hear you; he already has taken a dislike to you, and if he has a problem, you will be beaten again. That may kill you, this time."

Suddenly, he realized he could feel bruises and cuts all over his body, his bones feeling as if they had been battered with sticks. "Where...am I?" he asked. His tone was as dazed as he felt.

"Why you are in the Disciplinary Ward of the Station military hospital. Don't you remember?" she asked. She put a cold hand on his forehead and frowned. "You have had fever, but no delirium. At least, not until now."

"Oh. Yes, I remember now. Thank you." He sank back onto the foul-smelling tick of the pillow and thought hard. But before he could ask anything more, she turned to a patient on a cot at the other end of the room. He was beginning to moan and grunt, and she gave him one of the capsules, which calmed him at once.

Standish was thinking desperately. He could not be here in the hospital, not even the real one, and certainly not in this filthy place that was evidently for those intended for execution. Even as he thought that, the door opened and a sergeant entered. The face turned toward him, and he felt a jolt of recognition.

Gottenrod! He almost said the name, before he thought how dangerous that might be, here in this place. His old lover had no reason to think well of him. To be at his mercy was a thought that made even Standish cringe and try to hide beneath the filthy covers.

"So you've waked up, have you?" The familiar voice had a new edge of bitter hatred in it. "Good. We can play our little game again, can't we?"

Standish, staring up into those mad eyes, saw the resentful glare that he had put there, along with worse things, and he groaned. Was there no action whatsoever that did not come back to haunt you? He had abused Gottenrod in all the pleasurable ways he could think of for years. He had thrown him out, at the last, with bitter contempt. Now that emotion looked back at him from the face of the man who had been his lover.

"Groan away," the sergeant said. "Here, now...," and he brought up the staff he had been carrying and began thrashing it across Standish's body, which was still painful from the earlier beating.

The Commander groaned and tried to shield himself with his hands, but that was even more painful. His hands had been used for such protection before and were masses of contusions. When the man finished at last, Standish was once more in darkness, floating far from anything he knew. But he came to himself at once when someone lifted him and dropped him heavily onto a surface that was at once cold and knobby.

He found to his surprise that his eyes seemed to be stuck open. He couldn't even blink. The nurse was standing beside the cart on which he lay, checking off names, and the sergeant was double checking them. He was being sent away with those who had died in the night! He tried to speak, but nothing came from his dried throat. He tried to blink, as the nurse looked his way, but the stubborn eyelids would not move. His eyeballs felt hard and dry, frozen open.

"All accounted for," said the sergeant. "Take 'em away." There was an expression of sublime contentment on his rugged face.

"No!" cried Standish, but the shout could not pass his lips. He felt himself trundled off over rough and frozen tracks, and at last there was forest around him, trees bare, a track covered with drifts of fallen leaves. He found himself sweating with fear, as the cart drew up beside a pit. Even in the cold morning, there came from it a stench so overpowering he felt that he might faint.

The men who had brought him there paused to drink from a bottle. Then they began pulling stiff bodies from the other end of the cart. Standish lay there, unable to move, unable to speak, unable to do anything but let tears flow from his wide open eyes down into his cold ears, until he was flung into that noisome mess of composted human flesh, to sink into a mass of maggoty corruption.

* * * * * * *

Lilias, in her disguise as the serving woman, stood in the corridor, ostensibly dusting the ornamentation of the door. But she was listening to the sounds from the Commander's rooms. Jeroboah was correct. The drug he had provided was effective. Triggered by his appearance as a holographic image, the implanted hallucinations must be very real, to judge by the sounds from beyond the door. Best of all, as the tea and the cakes cooled, all evidence of the stuff vanished; no matter how they were analyzed, no trace could ever be found.

She turned from the door at last, carrying her tray, and limped down the corridor toward the kitchens. The Commander, it was already rumored, had a mental problem. He saw things that were not there at all. This, if it were mentioned, would reinforce that rumor. And even if he said nothing to anyone, changes were occurring in his look and his behavior.

Lilias chuckled. Her work had just begun.

CHAPTER TWENTY

PLOTTING COURSES

General Coville had no room to pace properly, but he stumped back and forth between his work table, the fire pit, and the end of Falville's bunk. His iron-gray hair was long now, and his beard had grown to respectable proportions, hiding his bony jaw, and providing a layer between his skin and the sharp wind that raked the mountains.

Falville, lying quiet in his bunk, watched his commander, knowing the older man was both worried and unsure. If they could only strike now, in the dead of winter when no one expected any movement from the rebel force, it could make the difference between triumph and defeat. But they were cut off, here in this tiny valley, enclosed by soaring peaks that were smothered in snow. To get out would be the work of a mountaineer of great skill, and to move the bulk of the army that rested here would be completely impossible.

As if reading his thought, Coville turned and stared down at him, managing not to flinch when he looked into his half-melted face. "I wish I knew what Seleva Karmann is up to," he said, his voice still gravelly with the remnant of a cold he had been fighting for a week. "And I wish I knew what those stiff-necked woodsmen will do when the time comes. And I know I sound like my small son used to, wishing for things I have no control over." He sighed deeply, then coughed.

Falville swung his feet over the edge of the bunk and sat, still moving carefully, though he now had a secure covering of scar tissue that made motion less painful than it had been two months before. He stretched cautiously, one arm, the other, then both legs. "I believe I could get out of here, General," he said.

"Give me Shoye and a couple of your best climbers, and I think we can make it down into Ellanish, at the least. That is downhill much of the way, once we get past the heights and valleys around us, and the slopes aren't as sheer as those on the western side of the range. I've been working out with the armsmaster, and he tells me I'm pretty fit again."

Coville stared at him for a moment, and Falville could see him thinking hard. Then the officer shook his head. "You haven't gained enough strength yet. How could you possibly get down the mountain, much less find Seleva in the woods and fields of Ellanish?"

"Shoye and the doctor say I am able. I'm still a bit tender in spots, but the cold will numb me, as I move. I'm going quietly crazy here, General. And I think I can find Seleva Karmann. We talked, while she nursed me on Stormwall. She told me things I remember, and that may give me a guide to her location. Besides which, I will make a wager she has made contact with our commando units there."

The young man said nothing about the bouts of pain that attacked him at night, making him feel as if all his muscles were being drawn into knots. Those were his own problems. He suspected violent exercise might ease him, anyway.

Coville turned away to the table, on which a tallow lamp guttered, making almost more smoke and fumes than reddish light. "I'll think about that," he said, as he bent to blow out the flicker of flame.

Falville stared into the darkness, listening to the breathing of the General, his aide Remarien, and the evil whistle of the wind around the curves of the hide and log shelter. He liked the darkness now. In daylight, when he chanced to glimpse a reflection of his scarred cheek and forehead, his seared ear, and his drawn eye, he shuddered. He closed his eyes when he bent over his washing bowl, and he didn't look into the cups of hot grain drink that were served with meals. The shifting images he saw there did nothing to comfort him.

There seemed to be nothing but his duty left for him. A life of his own, in a world no longer troubled by the ambitions of the Commander, would have included a wife and children, as well as his work on the farm that his family had planted for three generations. What woman would have him now? He had seen the involuntary shrinking, even of the men who had been his comrades, when they looked into his fire-washed face. He would never inflict such feelings on anyone, he felt, even if she seemed willing.

He could, instead, find a way to die that would help his people. It seemed to be the best way for him to go. Getting down the mountain would be the first step toward that.

A gust of wind almost shifted the hut on its foundation of boulders and logs. The banked coals in the fire pit glowed, as it sucked air up the chimney from the room, and in that dim glow, Falville saw that Coville was still awake, staring at the ceiling as he had done. So. He was truly thinking about sending a detachment down into Ellanish to make contact with Karmann and Lemmon. It might be that they could, if contact could be held, wait for one of the infrequent thaws that marked winters in Granary's northern hemisphere and, using information and allies that Seleva might have found, attack Station or one of the stronger outposts. Unexpectedly.

Triumphantly?

Falville sighed, and Coville said, very softly, "I think I may let you go. With about six men. And another half dozen may go back into Tellich. I want to locate Strindberg and find out what he is doing."

Falville found he had been holding his breath. Now he let it out in one long exhalation. "Thank you, Sir," he said. Then, as if permission had been given, he fell into a deep and restful sleep.

* * * * * * *

The General had good maps of Ellanish. The mountain range was shown in detail; the eastern coastline was even marked with depths of the various coves and anchorages. The main road, leading from Station northward to Sterne Rift, would be an infallible guide, for it had to be crossed to reach the eastern part of that country.

The outpost where the road leading to the coast and the port of Colyer crossed the north-south way was clearly shown to be the key to travel through Ellanish. The woodlands were so thick and impassable east of the road, and the spurs of the mountains extended so deeply into the fields on the west, that the road must be considered the only way to move troops either north or south.

There was no pass marked on the map. "Because there is no good route over the Gray Mountains, by summer or by winter," Coville explained, running his finger over the pattern of peaks and valleys. "No two valleys are connected by a passable stream bed. Not one of the heights has an easy route around it. The range can be crossed, but it takes terrible effort and determination. Nobody is going to expect anyone to come down from here in the winter."

He stared about him, from Shoye to Falville, from Rebman to Cannor to Frobish to Gall. "I want you to understand your worst danger will come from exposure and from the mountains themselves. If you get to Ellanish, you will find that the Station troops there will seem tame by comparison."

Falville nodded, and the others ducked their heads. More than one rebel was finding the winter insufferable here on the height. "I believe Seleva went this way," he said, touching a spot on the map that lay east of the road, southeast of their present location, and north of the outpost at the crossroad.

"She mentioned having friends who used to live in that area. If they are still there, she may have found help. And even if not, she said there was a big farmhouse that might be a possibility as a hiding place, for it was entirely out of the way, invisible if you didn't know where to go to find it."

Coville stared at the point where his finger rested. Then he glanced down at the outpost, marked with the sketch of a palisade. "If I know that lady, she and Lemmon will have interesting plans for the stockade," he said. "Yes. Go that way. If she is there, fine, and if not, you are in the area where she will be found, I am certain."

It required three days to equip the expedition with the best boots, the warmest clothing, and the lightest and best of the portable weapons that Coville's people had brought from Stormwall. The daily workouts that Shoye had imposed upon everyone in the encampment repaid his efforts, for even Falville was able to work alongside the uninjured, without growing wearier than they did. And when the work was done, the young officer found they were very well served.

Aside from weapons, food, and supplies, they were taking with them two long, slender sleds, formed from dried birch wood. The possibilities were obvious and exciting. If they found a long and unimpeded sweep of slope, deep in snow, they might cut off days of painful downward plodding. A rush down a mountainside—it had been decades since he had sledded, but he knew it would be well worth the effort of carrying the makings, if they found a chance to use them.

However, the climb out of the valley was something to forget as quickly as possible. The valley was a cup, and the walls of the circling cliffs curved inward like the lip of a vase. The only entryway was a hidden cut that curved over and under and around, so intricately that not even the most eagle-eyed flyer could spot the path.

The trip up that looping cut, impeded by many feet of snow, was something that Falville felt, ever afterward, had been a nightmare. Reality was not a part of it, though pain and exhaustion were. Many times, one or another of the group slipped and went shooting back down the chute, to be stopped only by the ropes attaching him to his companions. Falville fell twice, but he did not feel any shame at that. Shoye fell four times, much to his disgust.

They came out at the top of the cliffs after toiling for seventeen hours almost straight up, over snow that had thawed and refrozen enough times to be as slick as solid ice. Falville felt as if he had been rolled under the tracks of a carrier, and he knew the others felt the same.

They camped in a clump of boulders and Shoye built a fire. "No one but a bunch of idiots is up here to see," he said, when Falville objected. "And we'll do no manner of good if we're frozen corpses in the morning. There are times, young man, when caution is reckless, and this is one of 'em." Then he struck his flame; the pitch-wood he had brought with him in his pack flared to life.

They rose before first light, and Falville knew he was not the only one who was sore and stiff and still weary. But they headed eastward toward the paling gray of the sky, and by the time the sun rose over the farther peaks they had come down a long distance and were traversing another valley, this one long and narrow. Climbing out of it, when the time came the next day, was even worse than leaving their own had been.

Valley followed valley, height followed height, and day followed day. They killed a hornbeast to supplement their food supply, and they ate the meat raw, blood running down their sleeves to drip, in dark red splotches, on the snow. That brought their energies back to strength, and they traveled more quickly, climbing, falling, skidding, sliding, and slogging through the drifts.

Eight days after leaving the valley, Falville found himself standing on a ridge so narrow and rocky that not even the persistent snow could stick there. Below was a long sweep of white, curving smoothly to meet the edge of a wide span, the edge of one of the famous fields of Ellanish. They had passed through the mountains without a single man lost.

Even as he thought it, there came a gasp from behind him. He turned to see Shoye stagger and slump forward. Before he could reach the man's side, Rebman had dropped to his knees in the snow and caught the old man in his arms.

"What?" asked Falville, also kneeling and looking into the weathered face.

"Too old," the quartermaster sighed. "Thought I was still young, I did. But just too old. Sorry. Tell the Gen...," and then he was gone, his eyes empty of life.

Stunned with the suddenness of loss, Falville looked about at the four solemn faces in the snow. Shoye had been a constant reassurance that there was someone who knew the terrain, knew the drill, knew the way to do anything necessary. And now he was gone, and Falville knew only he had any idea what must be done next.

He rose from his knees and looked down at the blank face, the lax body, the yellow stain of urine coloring the snow. "We must hide him carefully. We're too near that outpost to take any chances—they probably send patrols up here from time to time. Gall, you and Cannor find a rocky spot that we can mark, yet which will hide his body. Rebman, you and Frobish lift him and take him with the others. I will...cover the marks."

As he swept snow over the stains, Falville felt tears freezing on his cheeks. He told himself his eyes were tearing with the cold, but he knew better. Shoye had been his father's comrade, his own trainer, and a staunch friend. He would miss him for many reasons, not the least of which was the task he must now accomplish without the aid of that knowledgeable guide.

CHAPTER TWENTY-ONE

AND THE WALL CAME TUMBLING DOWN

Yace was tired. He had worked at digging and shoring up the tunnel beneath the wall of the military post for a long while. Then he had gone trudging through the countryside, organizing the small groups of holdouts who hid in the woods and the edges of the mountains.

Fresto's group was nearest, and he found them without too much trouble. Killek, like the bear he resembled, had his people hidden in the deeps of a particularly overgrown forest, and it took hours of whistling the signal to call up a guide. Lister, with her usual silent intuitiveness, met him as he returned from that foray and assured him her force was waiting, ready for the attack on the fort. He thought he would not want to be among those she attacked, for her eyes glinted with controlled ferocity, and he recalled her saying that her parents had died at the hands of the very troop now in the compound.

Darwood was not to be seen, and Yace did not look for him. He did not trust that young fellow, for some unnamable reason. The longer he stayed away, the better it was for everyone.

Yace had returned to the farmhouse to find everything in readiness for the attack. There was little to do now except wait. Seleva, in the long day that must be endured before they took their places, had taken great interest in Jon, questioning him repeatedly.

At last, she took the boy into one of the many rooms on the ground floor of the house, carrying with her the strange box she kept always attached to her belt. The two remained together for hours, and from time to time Yace could hear the boy's voice, very weary and desperately sad. When Seleva Karmann returned to the others who waited in the huge living room, she was pale as paper. She walked with great care, as if she were made of glass and the least jarring step might shatter her small body to fragments. The thing on her belt, which had been silver colored, now was a different hue, tinged with scarlet.

"It is full," she said to Lemmon, who looked puzzled. "Even if there is more suffering to be gathered, there is no room for it. Jeroboah did not know, when he invented this thing, to what use it would be put. Or did he?"

Lemmon looked as puzzled as Yace and the others felt. She had heard no word, ever, of the use she intended for that box. The name of Jeroboah was totally unfamiliar to them.

Yace wondered if the old woman was coming apart under the stress of her efforts against Theron Standish. It could not be easy for even the most unforgiving grandmother to assist in the destruction of her grandson.

Now, waiting in hiding for the time to arrive, he took the opportunity to rest, while keeping his ears attuned to the forest around him. It was filled with people, though there was nothing to indicate that. Seleva, just beyond the great bole of the tree at his right, breathed so lightly that he looked around the trunk, from time to time, to see if she still lived. But she seemed able to rest in almost any position or situation.

Lemmon, beside her, was always alert when his face appeared. She seemed untroubled by the long wait before them. It had been her suggestion that they get into position the evening before their intended attack, waiting there in case the wall collapsed before Seleva expected it to. Even now, knowing the shoring beneath that wall had to be a raging blaze, sending its breath down the tunnel and into the wood, Yace could detect no hint of smoke. Their luck continued to hold.

He sighed and shifted his weight to the other hip. Jon, beyond a clump of bushes, pushed down a whisk of dried leaves and winked at him in the gathering dusk.

It was going to be a long night.

There was snow in the mountains, moving lower and lower all the time. The wind that swept down the slopes toward the east brought the bitter bite of the chill to those waiting in the wood. Yace huddled his blanket closer about Jon, who had curled close to him when darkness fell. The boy was a warm lump, and the blanket covered them both, but it was less than sufficient shelter from the chill of the night.

He lay there, his right side feeling a line of frost creeping into his bones, his stubborn eyes refusing to close. And then he heard something so familiar and yet so entirely unexpected that he stiffened in shock. Someone was moving through the wood, with quiet expertise yet without the desperate caution demanded by someone getting into position for an attack.

He loosed himself gently from the boy and crept, weapon ready, from his spot and through the bushes. He almost collided with Lemmon, who was bent upon the same errand. He couldn't see her, but he recognized her characteristic wood smoke and soap scent in the darkness.

"Sssss!" she hissed, almost below the level of hearing.

He touched her shoulder, and they parted, moving to right and left to intercept the unknown intruder. When the one moving through the trees came directly between them, he and the woman moved simultaneously, taking him from right and left and covering his mouth, so no shout could disrupt the silence.

"Kill him!" panted Yace, struggling to hold the squirming body still, and finding himself hard put to keep knees and elbows and strong fingers from sensitive parts of his anatomy.

"No. May know something!" came the reply.

With great difficulty, they secured the prisoner. Then Lemmon moved away quietly, and Yace half carried his burden into the brush to the spot designated as a meeting place, in case of need. Backed by an outcrop of granite, which had been thrust high by some natural convulsion of nature, it screened torchlight from any point at which it might be visible from the road. It also sheltered anyone there from the increasingly bitter wind.

He found the spot by blundering into the rough wall of rock. Luckily the prisoner took the brunt of that, leaving Yace relatively unscathed, and they waited in the darkness for Seleva to come. She arrived quickly; they lit a torch and thrust it into a narrow cranny to shed illumination on the questioning that all of them knew must come. But when the light picked out the features of the captive, Seleva drew a quick breath of recognition.

"Are you not Nedra, the wife of Arvid Strindberg?" she asked, her tone unbelieving. "I saw you only from a distance and in firelight, but surely it is you. What are you doing here?"

"I came to find you, though I had no notion it would be so easy," replied the woman. "I was told where to come by a man who escaped from Station—a man named Durk, who said he was the son of one Darrell, now dead. Coville sent word that someone would be raiding the crops here by the time you arrived. It seems he knew what he was talking about."

"Why did he send you?" asked the old woman. Her parchment-like face seemed suddenly weary and worn.

"We have found a way into Station," said the woman, dropping to sit on a knee of rock. "Is it safe to talk here? And why are you perched in the forest like a batch of carrion birds?"

"That later. A way into Station? I doubt that very much. My grandson is so wary, even the garbage carts are searched, going and coming. I shudder to think what traps and tripwires there may be for anyone approaching his Stronghold. There is no way for anyone without special knowledge to approach his command post without being caught."

"Durk escaped. He is leading Arvid and our force back along his track, even now, to approach the Stronghold from a completely unexpected direction. We want to find a ruse that will bring the bulk of the Station troops out of the city, so we can deal with Standish on somewhat more equal terms."

"A ruse? How would the loss of the Ellanish outpost serve to pull off such a trick?" asked Lemmon.

Nedra stared at her, then at Seleva. "Is this why you camp in a winter wood at night?" she asked.

Seleva nodded. "Tomorrow, we should be inside the post."

The woman smiled grimly. "Allow a group to escape and take the word back to Station. That is surely not a thing rebels would want, and it should trick the Commander nicely. Once troops move north along the road, Arvid will pinch shut the passage. They will not be allowed back into the city."

She glanced at Lemmon. "There is a way to jam any transmission telling of the attack?"

Lemmon nodded. "We have a communicator that Falville reprogrammed to match the frequencies of the command channel used by Standish's troops. We can broadcast a signal that will overlap any messages on the channel over a relatively small radius. But that should be enough to keep those in the outpost from getting a signal for help back to Station, for we have it in place in the forest south of the compound."

Yace found his mind racing. He had never thought himself particularly quick of wit, before his world fell into the hands of the Commander of Station. Now, however, he found he was following the thinking of those who were planning these moves. But there was one question that was unanswered.

"How are you going to get into the Stronghold? I was told there are mechanical guardians that no one can trick, weapons and systems Standish can control at a distance, as well as sensors that pick up motion or body heat. And there is nobody inside to open the gates or to disable the devices."

"Isn't there?" Nedra looked both grim and knowing. "The answer might surprise many, including the Commander."

* * * * * * *

If Yace had found it difficult to sleep before the interruption, it was impossible to doze off after it. Curled for warmth around Jon's skinny body, he kept thinking of the coming morning. The fire still burned. They had a group in position behind the post, waiting to attack it from the rear and keeping an eye on the progress of the blaze. No, the fire would burn out the shored tunnel, that was certain.

But would Seleva's device work? He had never heard of such a manner of removing a wall. However, farmers were seldom called upon to take down the walls of forts, so he hoped this was just one of the many things he had missed in his scanty education. Seleva herself seemed to have no doubt as to its effectiveness.

Light touched the sky above the treetops at last, and Jon stirred, waking Yace from an uneasy doze. "Is it time?" the boy asked in a whisper.

"Just about," the young man replied, turning back the blanket and stretching his cramped limbs. "Get something to eat from my pack. And be quiet!"

That was unnecessary, and he knew it. Jon had sworn never to be taken alive again by the troops who had abused him. He had told Yace enough, in the days they had known each other, to persuade the older boy he never wanted to hear the entire story of the child's captivity. Useless fury, he had learned already, did nothing but eat away at your heart.

Lemmon came around the tree and grunted. Yace rose and went with her to kneel beside Seleva, whose concealed position commanded the only view of the fort. Screened by a thicket of bramble and berry bushes, she could watch the front gates, and now she pointed and moved aside to allow him to look.

Breakfast fires were alight inside. He could see the smoke rising into the still air. He knew the troops were grumbling over their morning wash-up in cold water and their inspection of arms. The nozzles of flamethrowers and laser cannon were visible, if he searched the walls closely, as dark dots among the rough logs.

Seleva nodded, and Lemmon vanished silently. It was time to get the attack force into position. Facing those devilish weapons was nothing any of them wanted to do, but Yace was hoping with all his might the distraction from the rear (where he had seen for himself that there were very few weapons emplacements) would take the pressure off those attacking.

And now, for the first time, the wind changed, a puff of breeze coming off the distant sea to bring the tang of dry smoke to Yace's nose. As he took his place in concealment, beside Lemmon and not too far from Jon, he began to quiver with excitement. He had known danger, but it had been of the kind that comes unexpectedly and is dealt with almost offhandedly, without the time to worry and wonder beforehand.

This was his first battle, and he felt his chest tighten with the tension. Seleva, ahead of him and to his right, seemed taut as a bowstring, and he thought her pale face was even whiter than usual as they waited for the time to creep past and the wall to come down.

He could feel, as well, the taut anticipation of those hidden in the wood about him. Not one was convinced that he or she would live to see this day's sun set behind the mountains.

The sun rose behind a thin veil of cloud, and the wind gusted uneasily, first from the east, bringing smoky breaths from the forest, then from the west, chilling their backs with the wind off the snowfields.

The orderly progression of the military day behind the walls continued. Orders were shouted, drills were held, accompanied by the clashing of boot heels and the clanking of weapons. It was too late for the troops there to do any work toward securing their supplies for the winter. The crops were burned or carried away and hidden in secure places. Most of the noncombatants had taken the advice of the agents sent by General Coville and had moved to hidden valleys in the mountains, so there were few slaves to be seized from the farmsteads.

The soldiers had to amuse themselves with military occupations, and little joy did they seem to take in that. And then, as Yace watched breathlessly from the treetop he had chosen as his perch, the wall along the northern side of the post began to sag. Just visible beyond the parade ground from his elevated position, the center of the bastion hesitated, sagged even more, hesitated again. Then it plunged downward, along with a good span on either side, and a gust of dark smoke went up in a rush.

There came a cry of alarm, but Seleva held up her hand, and a flight of arrows sang over the wall and into the invisible ranks of Station troops. They trailed smoke, and when they hit the shake roofs of the barracks lines, the dry wood blazed up instantly. Others, landing behind the wall, brought shouts and screams from those caught in the barrage.

That caught the attention of the commanders inside at once, and as they shouted orders, the attacking force yelled with all their might. They ran toward the gates, volleying arrows and hurling stones, hoping to divert those inside from any thought of their collapsing wall.

It took only a moment for the trained soldiers to get into position, but Seleva's move was, of course, only a feint. She kept her people yelling and darting forward and back to throw stones or shoot arrows, before running again into the shelter of the wood. They lost few, though from time to time Yace had to step over a prone body or pause to support an addled companion into the wood.

Yace yelled with the rest, hurling stones and pounding at the gates with the strength born of unbearable tension. He found himself strangely unafraid, now the moment had come. He was able to hurl himself into the dreadful chaos of searing laser beams and spattering gusts of flame from the mounted throwers, without any thought for his own skin. Even when he had to leap over a blazing body, frying in its own fat, he managed not to think this might have been himself, if he had gone left instead of right.

Smoke billowed from many sources. The clouds obscured the entire clearing, beginning to sift down thin drifts of snowflakes, now. That made the attackers feel somewhat safer, as they darted forward and back, eluded licking tongues of fire, and dragged their injured or dead companions back into the shelter of the wood. But the space between wall and trees was now beginning to be littered with their casualties.

When the wall sank at last into a billow of flaming debris, those who had waited in the eastern wood attacked at last, leaping over the smoldering masses of soil and timber. Yace could hear their cries and he imagined the terror of falling into that inferno. But the unexpected assault diverted the attention of the troops facing the road. A group of Killek's people dug in at the forest's edge to harry them with arrows from the wood, as the rest prepared to make the crucial assault.

With the rest of Seleva's people, Yace fell back and came around to the north to assist the fresh group. He found himself staggering blindly over stones that his own people had cast from their improvised catapults, stepping onto the bodies of men who had been stunned by the barrage. Others were skewered with arrows, and he blessed the smoke and the blowing snow that hid their dead eyes from his gaze.

Orders were shouted into the murk, but it was hard for the soldiers to tell friend from enemy now. Firing blindly, they took out as many of their own as of the attackers, and they soon began to fall back behind the portable laser cannon. Borne forward by the fury of their private losses, the enraged farmers fought their way through the compound. They had the advantage of the snow and the smoke, and in time they cut the troops into small pockets, cornered and disarmed the bulk of them.

Yace was burdened with prisoners and captured weapons, as the compound was secured. He hoped Lemmon had been able to distort any transmission reporting the attack.

The smaller gate was unbarred, but the rebels pretended not to notice that in the confusion. The First Officer and his aide escaped, pounding away down the road on feet that seemed to have sprouted wings. Watching them go, Yace chuckled softly, and Seleva, her pale face grimed and weary, did the same. Nothing could have seemed more natural, and when the pair, days later, would come limping into Station, Yace felt Standish would not doubt for a moment that their escape was just what it seemed to be. He had never questioned his good fortune in matters of war, his grandmother assured her followers.

CHAPTER TWENTY-TWO

TIME FOR GOING HOME AGAIN

The outpost was secured almost too easily, once the soldiers knew their commander had fled. By that time the fugitives were out of sight, and the snow had thinned to an occasional flurry. The wounded were carried into temporary shelter before anything else was attempted. The dead were laid in a long row at the edge of the forest, leaving the compound itself clear for work parties.

Instead of trying to man the partially unwalled fort, which would have been a task uncongenial to the farmers of Ellanish, Yace led his people in taking the place apart, timber by timber, pole by pole. The materials were carted away on the backs of men or on handcarts taken from the supply sheds.

Jon worked beside his friend, and Seleva sat on a pile of stacked lumber and supervised the disassembly of her grandson's fort. She was tired. Too tired for even that light work, but she knew if she did not remain busy and alert, she would collapse. There was still work for her to do, before she could allow that to happen.

The device, still attached to her belt, was a constant distraction, filling her body and her mind with pain, but she did not remove it and lay it aside. Things were too easily lost in such unsettled times, and she had suffered too much in acquiring the intensities of agony that now existed within the thing that Jeroboah had made. She and it had to arrive together at the Stronghold, some time in the very near future.

She thought of the fugitives, even now sprinting away toward their leader with their warning. The snow clouds had now blown away eastward, and the watery sun would speed them on their way.

She must move and soon. The troops from Station would be on the road within a week, while she must go the long way around, avoiding any chance of discovery by those who had, she knew quite well, been sent out by her grandson to find her and bring her back into his area of control. The road to Station would be one continuous pitfall. She knew she could not go up into the skirts of the mountains. Snowstorms raged there that were quite visible, still, from the valley of Ellanish. She could never survive the intense cold, the taxing climbs and descents that would be required for that route. She had to find someone to accompany her through the forest toward her home.

Yace? She shook her head. He was a strong boy, growing wiser every day, but he was needed with his own people. Jon, in particular, had attached himself to the older boy, and would be devastated if he had to be left behind. And this would be no journey for a child. Or for an old woman!

She chuckled wryly at the thought. She had longed, in her late middle age, for a time of peace in her latter years. A time when she could look back and sort out her life and her actions, acknowledging those that were necessary and good, as well as those that were altogether evil and unnecessary.

Every human being had the right to mend her soul, she had thought. To winnow out the debris of her life and actions, her necessity and anger and impatience. She had not been altogether wise or even principally well-meaning, and she understood that better with every day she lived. She had done things that now filled her with cold despair, and she needed the time to come to terms with them. But there had been no time.

Theron had robbed her of her old age, even as he had robbed her people of their freedom, their lands, and their lives. If nothing else, she had dedicated herself to preserving autonomy for every group and Grange and settlement of people on Granary, after their long years of servitude under the Governors imposed upon them by the Consortium of the United Worlds.

The revolution she had led had thrown out those self-serving officials and their even more self-serving principals. The contract she had wrested from the Traders had given this, of all the agricultural worlds, the opportunity to show what a free people, managing their own affairs, could accomplish. Now her own flesh and blood was intent upon restoring the old slaveries to the world he intended to control from sea to sea, and from Wheatlands in the north to the stony deserts to the south of the citrus growing orchards.

She sat on the stack, her shoulders sagging with the burden she carried. Someone must come to take her to Stronghold to carry her bodily, if need be, before her exhaustion felled her body or damaged her mind. Even as she thought that, a hail sounded from the road. She stared over the hip-high remnant of the wall, which was disappearing pole by pole even as she looked, and saw a tattered group coming through the light drifts of snow from the wood. Something about their leader caught her eye, and she stood to see better.

Falville. She knew his long-legged walk, the carriage of his head. The scars were invisible at such a distance, but she could see that he moved well and easily. Good. He deserved to heal from his terrible injuries. She hoped he would be able, in time, to build a good life for himself when this struggle was done.

She called softly, and Jon came from Yace's side to see what she wanted. "Go and tell those men to come to me, Jon. I need them, and here they are! Call Lemmon, too. We need to talk."

The boy ran toward the four men, leaping easily over the remnant of the wall. They stopped as he came up to them, his hands waving as he told them where to go and who had asked to see them. Then Falville turned his head fully into the light, and her heart caught in her throat. Half of his face had melted and run like wax, leaving his eye as a haunted hollow above the ruin. She remembered his agony, as she interacted with Jeroboah's pain trap. She could see the reflection of it in him, a shadow coloring all that he was and ever would be. Even if his body should heal miraculously, leaving him unscarred, he would carry the memory with him forever.

Now the men moved toward her, and she could see by the droop of their shoulders and the swing of their legs that they had traveled long and hard. As they neared her, she sent Lemmon, newly arrived from her task of overseeing the damping out of all traces of the fire beneath the wall, after wine and food from the kitchens, which had been left until last for destruction.

"Well, my friend, you have healed more quickly than I ever would have dreamed," she said, as Falville bent over her hand and greeted her.

"They found another store of false skin. They used it on me, for Coville needed me. It allowed healing to progress more quickly than usual. It also prevented stiffness and thick scarring. But it did nothing for my beauty." His tone, strangely, was not bitter.

Lemmon came with a dusty bottle and a plate of hard bread and dried fruit. She did not flinch when she looked into the scarred face of her old friend. "They were already feeling the pinch," she said. She set the food on a nearby stack and passed out the bottles. "Things were going to get very sticky before the winter was out. We did them a favor, and now we will have to feed the captives. I suspect before we are done we'll add them to our own troops. They are a scarred and sorry bunch."

"Mistreated and misled," Seleva agreed. "Theron specializes in ill-treating those who help him. But there is no time for gossip. I must move before I am too exhausted to travel. Falville, are you able to help me get to Station?"

He raised his head, the sun striking mercilessly across his ruined face. "I came through the mountains. I survived losing Shoye. After that, I think I can do anything that is necessary."

Lemmon gasped with shock, setting a bottle on the stack and sinking down beside it. Her strong hand clasped Seleva's, but she didn't interrupt him with questions.

"I can get you to Station, Seleva Karmann. Are you ready to go now, or will you wait until tomorrow, when we have all had some rest?"

"I should go now. But neither you nor I will do our best, if we push too hard. We will rest tonight in the house of my friend Darrell, may peace be with his memory. And tomorrow we will start fresh. We must avoid the road. Troops will come back this way in only a few days, for we allowed some to escape. That serves a plan made by Arvid Strindberg, who sent his wife to tell us. We must travel through the forest, and we must go quickly." She felt even more weary, knowing what a contradiction in terms that was. The forest resisted travelers fiercely and at every step.

Falville sighed. He knew the terrain across the mountains, but here in this thickly wooded country, he did not. This was not going to be an easy task, without a guide who knew the most accessible routes.

A small voice piped up, almost under his elbow. "I know the way. I came from Station a long time ago, with my mother and father. We came through the forest—we lived very near it and knew it, and it sheltered us as we ran. It was only bad luck the troops were out cutting wood and caught us. That was when they took me into their fort and...."

Seleva put her hand on the boy's head and turned it so she could look into his eyes. "You are safe, now, Jon. You can stay here with Yace, and help get the fields and the houses and the people back into their normal condition. You don't have to put yourself in danger again. I would not ask it of you. And Yace will want you near him. He feels you are a small brother, I think."

"Yace is my friend. I'll come back to him, but if you need someone to show you how to go, then you need me. I will go. If I can do anything to hurt that man in Station, I want to. His men...his men killed my father and did terrible things to my mother until she died. And then they did them to me, but I didn't die. If I can hurt them, I will."

The small face, grubby from the smoke and soot and the dusty timbers he had helped to move, was set, older by far than its years. His chapped lips were set with a purpose suitable to one far older than he.

Seleva nodded. Such determination was valuable to her, though she hated to take a child back into the stronghold of her grandson. "Then Yace must have a chance to come, too. Call him, will you Lemmon? My voice is too weak to make an impression on this din."

The mutter of talk, the clatter of wood on wood and metal on metal, did, indeed, make it hard to hear in the compound. So when Yace joined them, Seleva directed the small group to go at once to the house of Darrell again, where they could rest and refresh themselves, as well as talk in a secure spot, where listening ears and careless tongues were no risk.

As they went, she thought of the wounded, now carried away to the homes of the farmers. There was no sophisticated medical help for them, no specially designed burn treatments. She hoped devoutly that the herbal remedies the local people were learning to use would be of help to those now suffering the effects of Theron's wicked weapons.

* * * * * * *

Jeroboah had waited for years while Standish formed his armies, fortified his Stronghold, and tightened his iron grip on this newly hopeful world. Granary was by far the worse for his presence, and it was not hard even for one so absent-minded as the ancient to remember that.

Seleva had taken his device.

That was a good thing, he thought, though often he didn't remember exactly why it was true. His interface with the Stronghold systems he had installed was a good thing too. He could deceive any piece of electronic equipment Standish relied upon to keep him safe and isolated from others. He could project holograms wherever he wanted, if he only could remember where and for what purpose.

The old man felt uneasy, however, his nerves twitching with the need for action; as yet the proper course had not occurred to him. Was he neglecting something vital? Was he allowing his old friend Seleva to waste her suffering and her life because his erratic mental processes were temporarily out of order?

He sat in his chair and touched buttons that brought his many screens to life. There was Standish in his quarters, bending over his table to study the disposition of his troops. There was the guard-room, where monitors picked up every angle of the surrounding gardens and the fields beyond their walls. He bent forward suddenly, recognizing among the officers on duty the face and shape of someone he recognized. The assassin Standish used. Cozarre. Now why would he be in the central control room of Stronghold?

There was Karmann, looking dispirited, going over long files of records and making occasional notes to bring to the attention of his cousin. A pity he had been a better man than his allegiance allowed him to show.

And there, on his own monitor that surveyed the north road, Jeroboah saw a quiver of motion in the distance. Men, limping along, but still hurrying toward Station. Their uniforms proclaimed them Station troops. One was an officer. He could see the electronic "key" that the officer used every few yards in order to deactivate Standish's safeguards for long enough to pass.

The old man sank back into his chair and watched as the Station guardsmen detected the newcomers and sent crawlers to meet them and bring them into the Stronghold. He smiled as the pair was brought to Karmann, who questioned them thoroughly, although not, in Jeroboah's judgment, very perceptively.

As the story came out, Jeroboah grinned more broadly. So the farmers up there in Ellanish were not the sheep-like and submissive folk the Commander had thought, were they? And the post that had seemed so secure was taken, partially destroyed.

It sounded, to his experienced ear, like the work of his friend Seleva. He had seen her take stubborn fortifications many years before, as she led her forces. This had her techniques written all over it. But why had she allowed anyone at all to escape? He thought about that for a time, as the refugees were fed and washed themselves and were taken to the Commander. And then he knew.

They were going to deceive Theron Standish, all unknowingly and unintentionally. He would bet his life on it. That too was the sort of thing Seleva would do. It was a pity, he knew, that her grandson had not joined his complementary talents with hers. Granary would then have become a truly extraordinary world, unlike any other colonized planet in the Consortium.

He mused for a moment, knowing he was about to take a long risk. For now was the time to activate the final links in his electronic chain. Now was the time to signal that woman, living disguised under the nose of her tormentor, that things were coming to a head. She must make ready her most appropriate weapon and then wait for developments.

And so must he, though it meant risking revealing his presence to Standish's detectors. He touched another button, and the interior wall of the hut, which seemed to lean against the hill against which it was built, moved aside, revealing an even more intricate complex of computers, equipment, and power sources.

The old man rose and moved stiffly into the room, blowing dust from the console before which he now sat down. When he touched the control button, the thing lit up with a thousand points of brilliance. When he keyed in the command he had saved for just this situation, those points fused into lines of energy. A grid formed, crisscrossed with his network of sensors.

On the shabby roof something stirred, as mud and ice slipped aside to fall below. A dish lifted, turned, shook slightly to sift the debris of years through its open mesh, and then turned its somehow threatening face toward the place where the Commander of Station was at that moment sending troops northward, stripping his guard to a minimum in order to do so.

CHAPTER TWENTY-THREE

A DESPERATE HURRY

Yace had thought things were settled. The troops were dislodged from the outpost, and any who were abroad in Ellanish could soon be captured or killed. Things would return to normal, so he could take care of Jon. He had already decided to set up housekeeping in the farmhouse, keeping it ready if Durk should happen to return to his home. He'd had his eye on the daughter of the Grangemaster for years, and he had a feeling she might join them in time.

He had never expected to be summoned by Seleva and Lemmon to such a weird consultation.

"You need not go, Yace. Jon volunteered and would not hear of remaining behind. Now he has told me why, and I understand, though I hate to take him within reach of my grandson. We will not think less of you, if you decide to remain here and help your people get things back into some kind of order."

Seleva was looking at him with those clear silver eyes, and as usual he found himself agreeing to do something he knew was foolhardy, if not downright insane. But there was no way he would allow Jon to go without him. And Jon was going, that was perfectly obvious to everyone.

Yace found himself impressed by Falville. Though the melted face had put him off, at first, the clear mind and stubborn will behind it soon roused his admiration. This was a man who could ignore his own pain and weariness, one to follow anywhere, if there was need.

"The five of us can go faster and less noticeably than a larger group could manage," Seleva was saying, her voice weary but firm. "I will not risk any more of our people, for this is something that must be done by one alone. If you can get me to the Stronghold, I will be in position to achieve the thing I have been working toward for months. If you, Lemmon, and Falville, Yace, and Jon will agree, it will be only this group that will start out for Station in the morning. Early."

Falville looked dubious. "Lady, it is going to be a dangerous journey. The forest has many who fled when the wall went down. I've been told a number of the enslaved people from the farms broke for the forest when that happened. Some will be good folk, simply heading for home. But I suspect there will be those who worked with the troops to enslave their own kind. There always seems to be that kind, no matter where they may be."

Yace nodded. "Several," he said. "I wouldn't want to meet any of them, either. Not unless there was time to stand and make a good fight of it." He thought of Jarek, but he kept that to himself.

"Which there will not be. Things are moving fast, my friends, and we must reach our goal as quickly as possible, avoiding any delay whatsoever." Seleva's voice held an edge of desperation, and for the first time Yace could see how very old and tired she had become, just in the days since he met her in this house in the darkness.

"The men who came with me will help the local people organize, in case the troops from Station come so quickly they don't realize they have been cut off from headquarters," Falville said. "That will relieve our minds on their account. They will create an ambush of a classical sort that should go down in the books as a textbook example, or I don't know my people. We will go through the trees, as you suggest, avoiding the road. Maybe, if we are very lucky, we can slip through without being seen."

Yace went to bed with those words ringing in his head. He had a dismal feeling that such luck was not going to be theirs, and when they rose in the darkness before dawn to hear rain on the roof, he was sure of it. His first step onto the broad porch sent him skidding onto his backside, and his curses were heartfelt.

"Here, let me hold onto you, Seleva." That was Falville's voice.

Yace crawled to the edge of the porch and swung his feet down to the icy grass below. Jon came scooting expertly across the expanse and landed with a crunch beside Lemmon, who had managed to skid without falling and had leaped to the ground ahead of them all.

"We are going to be able to slip by without being seen or heard?" asked Yace, as he got to his feet, rubbing his tailbone. "Not likely! This stuff is going to sound like someone bashing his way through a glass factory."

"It will be better as we go south." Seleva's tone was reassuring, though he could hear her teeth chattering. "And perhaps we will be the only fools out in this weather." He noticed how stiffly she moved as they set off into the forest.

For a long while, it seemed she might be right. They crushed and crashed through ice-loaded bushes whose tops bent toward the ground, making barriers that were loud and difficult to break through. They came at last to forest that had not been cut over, whose trees rose to great heights above relatively clutter-free ground. There they hurried, their steps quiet on the dry leaves that were only occasionally glazed with ice.

The shelter of the canopy above was welcome, and they traveled for half a day at top speed, occasionally pausing to check the compass Falville carried. Losing their direction was a thing they had no time to do. They camped that night in a small niche in a stone outcrop that rose beside a frozen brook. They even risked a campfire, for their feet were numb, and their hands, even tucked into their coat pockets or bound in their scarves, were half frozen.

Food needed no cooking, for they had brought only bread and cheese and dried meat, but they boiled a canister of water, which began as ice and melted in the small, hot blaze. When it boiled in the pot, they made an herb tea from a supply Lemmon carried always with her. It warmed them from the inside, and afterward they covered the fire and rolled up together in a compact wad of five bodies, holding what warmth there was among them.

The next day, they began coming out of the frozen area, though the air was still icy. Here it had snowed instead of raining, and they found they could avoid the patches that had found a way down to ground level beneath the trees. Leaving footprints behind was not a thing they wanted to do.

Another day passed, and they were drawing near the stream that marked the lower boundary of Ellanish. As they crept across a foot log, stepping carefully to avoid a dunking in the water beneath the thin skim of ice, Seleva held up a hand. Her head was up, her eyes searching the forest on their right.

Yace, in the middle of the log, stopped, feeling himself sway. Jon, surefooted as an animal, came up behind and steadied him. When Seleva beckoned, they came forward carefully, making no noise at all.

The five gathered in a clump of whinberry, their heads close together. "What?" That was Falville, his voice a mere breath of sound.

"I heard something back in the forest. A whistle that was no bird I know, and I have made a point of learning the calls of every sort in our forests. Spread out along the stream bank. Keep your weapons ready. I think we are about to be attacked, and that was a signal."

Her silver eyes were bright as steel, and her hand was gripping her weapon. The scent of danger had stripped away the veneer of age and fragility, and now Yace saw a glimpse of the revolutionary and the ruler she had been in her youth.

He breathed deeply, letting out the breath with caution. He was glad he was here on her side and not waiting in the brush to ambush her. She was not one to attack without long thought and planning. He had rethought all his attitudes toward the old, while following this formidable old lady.

Falville sent him with Jon to drop behind a slab of stone. Lemmon stayed with Seleva in the clump of whin, and Falville let himself down into the streambed amid a tangle of vines on which the old leaves had been frost-killed, drying on the vines into a concealing canopy. There came a long wait or was it just seemingly long? Yace could not decide. And then he heard a footfall amid the mulch of the forest. Another whistle shrilled through the chill. A mutter of talk could be heard off to the left, where the stream bent sharply.

They were coming. Yace watched, risking one eye over the slab of stone behind which he and the boy lay, his head concealed by a rough web of branches from another bush. And when he saw who stepped from behind a tree and began to move toward the log, he felt his heart begin pounding with anger and alarm and a terrible, fierce joy.

It was Jarek. He should have known someone as opportunistic as his old acquaintance and tormentor would find others of his own kind. He should have guessed that people of the same sort might well hide out in the forest, preying upon anyone passing by. But he had never dreamed he would have the chance to square his account with Jarek after his escape. That was something fortune seemed eager to drop into his lap. Dangerous though it might be to the mission they were attempting, he could not find it in himself to regret it.

Jon, tightly crammed against his side, whispered, "What is it, Yace? I feel you trembling." The boy raised his own head cautiously, trying to see through the brush. Then his breath, too, caught abruptly. "Jarek." It was the merest sigh.

No plan of action had been made. Yace had not been told to avoid conflict, though he knew better than to court it. Their mission was too important for such heroics. But every part of him, mind and body, longed to rise and leap the stream and tackle that bulky figure, to batter its face into a pulp, and to trample body and limbs until they lay limp and lifeless.

As if she could read his thoughts, Seleva turned her face toward him. She nodded once, very slowly and deliberately. Then she clicked her fingers quietly, and Yace saw Falville's hand, still clinging to the stone that braced him to lean above the ice, move, flicking a finger in acknowledgement.

Again Seleva nodded toward Jarek, and Yace, freed from his obligation to remain quiet, slid around the stone and down to stand beside Falville. He had moved as quietly as any serpent, and there was no sign that Jarek had noticed anything amiss. "Enemy," he mouthed at Falville. "Mine!"

The soldier touched his shoulder and pointed toward a runnel leading up the other side of the stream. A boulder in the middle of the ice offered a footing, precarious but possible, by means of which he might gain the other bank without risking a telltale splash.

Yace felt himself grinning savagely, but he was already moving, his feet sure on the half-frozen mud, landing solidly on the boulder, leaping again to the gravel beyond the icy water. And Jarek heard that. As Yace rushed up the runnel, the man turned his face toward him, eyes widening as he recognized his former victim. He raised the pellet weapon he held, but something zinged from behind Yace, and the thing spun from Jarek's hands. Seleva? Most likely.

Then he was on the overseer, sending him down backward as he plowed into him. His knees were in the belly, now leaner but no less muscular. His hands curled into fists and pounded the face beneath him. The square jaw bruised his knuckles, but the pain felt good and the feel of breaking teeth was even better.

But Jarek had regained his breath. His brawny hands were around Yace's neck, tightening, tightening, until the lighter man felt his head might burst. He flattened the nose below his own, feeling a splatter of blood on his face. He dug his knees into the body under him, straining to keep the bigger man from rolling over on top of him.

Yace heard, without noting it consciously, other feet pounding up, other weapons hissing or splatting. He was fighting for his life now, his eyes beginning to see only black and purple blots instead of the face of his enemy. With desperate strength, he heaved backward, breaking the grip about his neck and allowing his victim to roll free of his body. Gulping for breath, Yace lowered his head and plowed forward, butting Jarek's throat with the top of his skull.

Then the man was down again, and Yace felt about for something, found a hand-sized stone, and struck hard. The rock hit with a soggy sound, and the tense form beneath him went suddenly limp. He rolled to his feet and turned to face whoever might accompany

Jarek, but he saw only a pair of retreating backs and a still shape lying at the edge of the stream. Falville bent over it, taking its weapons, checking it for life, and then turning away, leaving it for the carrion eaters.

"Station lies only a few klicks to the south now," Seleva called. "Are you able to move, Yace?"

The boy was breathing hard as he felt himself all over. Except for bruises and fingernail cuts, he seemed to be well, and he nodded.

Jon came bouncing over the stream to bury his face in Yace's shirt. "I thought he would kill you! He's so big and so mean and so tough...he was one of them. One of the ones...."

Yace felt his face turn hot. He wished he could go back in time and kill the man more slowly. But he only patted the rough hair and said, "It's all right now. We've got to move, Jon. Which way do we go from here?"

CHAPTER TWENTY-FOUR

SARI

The days had stretched endlessly as winter wrapped Station in its grim chill. The Disciplinary Ward was colder than ever, its patients suffering from chilblains, where they were not bruised and cut. Sari thought each day that she could not endure one more morning of coming in to find stiffened corpses waiting to be listed on her tally. It wasn't in her to stop feeling sympathy for the wretches she nursed. Worse yet, there was nothing she could do for them. The only medication she was given was the pill to put them to sleep, and any effort she made to clean the place or her patients was met with hostility and threats from Gottenrod.

She thought the sergeant was watching her more closely than ever before. Was he beginning to suspect that not every corpse sent away in the cart was altogether dead? She became more cautious, trying to save only those that Gottenrod beat most viciously. Her dreams became curiously interwoven with her daily rounds, and she got little rest. She worked frantically, even in her sleep, to ease the inhuman treatment of those in her care.

Sometimes Sari wondered how someone only twenty-two years old could feel so ancient, so disillusioned, and so grim. The time came when she lost any fear of being caught at her nefarious work. What could death do that life was not doing more painfully? Men and women came and suffered and died, came and suffered and died, until Sari felt she had died those deaths herself. Gottenrod would have a hard time punishing a corpse, she decided, and so she went doggedly ahead with what she considered her duty as a Medic and a human being.

If the Commander of Station objected, let him face her with it. And even if he should, she would continue until they made her stop.

She could see as she washed her face each morning that lines were forming about her mouth and her dark eyes. There were strands of gray showing in the auburn of her hair. The happy girl she had been five years before had disappeared as if she had never been. She was growing old, for here every day was equal to at least a year. Her head ached when she rose and her heart ached when she went to bed again. Death, she thought, would at least make a change in her existence.

Often she wondered about those she had tried to save. Had any made it through alive? She thought again of the ones she had liked best. Anya. Probably she had died in the wood, if she had lived past the compost pit. Her injuries were internal, untreatable. But she was so young, and her eyes were so filled with longing for life! Sari had tried her best, knowing it was better to crawl into the forest and die like an animal than to breathe your last in the hellhole that was the Disciplinary Ward.

Kell had been strong still, although his bruises had made him look terrible. She felt he might well have made it out of Station. Durk...she smiled when she thought of the farmer boy. He had possessed a sunny nature that even his sufferings in the military had not succeeded in souring entirely. She hoped he still lived.

That was questionable, for Gottenrod had taken an especially harsh interest in the boy for some reason. His ordinary beatings were inhuman, and with Durk they went past even that. It was as if he saw in the youth something he had lost and could never regain.

She shook her head and opened the door of her room. The stink of the ward was something she seldom noticed now, for she was used to it. It was the two still, blue faces, open eyes staring at the dingy ceiling, that she could never accept, never grow accustomed to allowing to die without help. She checked the living first, doling out fresh water and sleeping pills to those in the most pain. The food cart would come at midmorning, and she thought it would be too late to nourish the woman in bed three and the boy in bed twelve.

The dead were Shipp and Lattery. She closed their eyes with gentle fingers and listed them on the tally. Already she could hear the dead-cart rattling over the pavement toward the door, and she went to meet the handlers. They were well on their way to drunkenness, and she didn't blame them. Theirs was a nasty job. The ward might be terrible, but once she had walked, in an off hour, through the wood to the pit. That was the most horrible thing she had ever experienced, and the memory of it never quite left her.

The lime did little to quell the stench. She could see elbows and knees, skulls with parts of faces still attached, rumps and shoulders protruding from the nauseous mess, all powdered with the omnipresent white of the quicklime. She shivered and looked up as Gottenrod followed the cart to the door of the hospital. He was looking particularly frightening this morning. Nothing pleased him as much as cruelty, and when her eyes met his she saw in his gaze something that made her suddenly go cold.

"And how is our little nurse this morning?" he asked. She would have preferred his usual growl to this saccharin tone. "Ready for a break in your duties? Ready to talk to the Questioner?"

Sari took a deep breath and braced her shoulders. She had known this day would come. She'd thought she was prepared, but now she wondered if anyone, ever, could prepare herself for what was certain to come now.

* * * * * * *

She had never been inside the Stronghold. The hospital where she had trained was in Station in the great white building constructed in the earlier days of the colony. Seleva Karmann had renovated it, equipping it with every sort of modern medical device and drug available from the Traders of her time. It was a good facility, and it turned out excellent doctors and dedicated nurses. Too dedicated, Sari thought now, as she went through the series of metal doors, each equipped with sensors and electronic locks that answered only to hand and voice-prints. If she had been less well trained, she might have been able to close her eyes and work by the book—that new book Theron Standish was in the process of writing for his people.

The corridors in the Stronghold were a maze, curving, forking, and recombining. She walked steadily, avoiding the hand that sometimes grasped her elbow from behind. She did not want Gottenrod's hands on her, no matter how briefly.

They came to a door that was painted dark brown, in contrast with the white ones that had lined all the corridors. On this the sergeant rapped once with the heavy ring on his right hand.

After a moment, there came the sound of electronic locks whining, as well as the rasp of bolts being withdrawn. "Who?" came a sexless voice through the speaker.

"I have the nurse. Is the Questioner ready?" Even the sergeant sounded somewhat subdued. Sari had never heard of the Questioner until recently, but she dreaded anyone who could make Gottenrod look cowed.

The door slid aside into the wall, and Sari stepped through, her head up, her eyes staring straight into the face of the tall woman who stood beside the inner doorway.

"I am ready, of course. There is nothing like one's duty to make one ready. And this is the nurse whom you accuse of...what? Suspicious concern for her patients."

The voice, deep and somehow disturbing, sounded amused. "In another time and place, you would be under suspicion yourself for such an accusation. But such is life. As one of the ancient races on old Terra used to say, 'other times, other ways.' Come in, child. I am Mora." She stepped back and ushered Sari into the inner chamber as politely as if she were a guest.

But when Sari realized what it was she was seeing, the chill she had felt earlier turned into a rigor that shook her from head to foot. There were the expected syringes and arrays of drugs for extracting the truth from the unwilling. There were electrodes with delicate clips formed for attachment to sensitive parts of the body. But there were also things she had not dreamed still existed in any world of mankind.

She was certain that in a corner beyond the surgical steel table she recognized a rack. The contraption of ropes and straps and pulleys that swung from the ceiling was surely a nasty device she had seen in one of the forbidden books she had scrutinized with serious attention when she was twelve. A chum had filched it from her father's library. *Journal of the Marquis de Sade* was its title, and Sari still felt the frisson of horror that the diagrams and sketches had given her. What had that thing been called?

"The strappado," she said aloud, her tone surprisingly calm. "Used by the Marquis de Sade. Surely no device for the use of civilized people." She shuddered, thinking of being dropped from the height of the tall ceiling, only to be brought up short, some distance from the floor, by the rope attached to arms tied together behind her. Her shoulders ached at the thought.

The woman smiled warmly, her wrinkles springing into high relief. "My dear child, what a delight to find a victim so well versed in esoterica. Of course these are not the tools of civilized societies. But, dear child, this is by no means a civilized society. Hadn't you noticed?"

And then Sari began to shiver in earnest.

CHAPTER TWENTY-FIVE

CONJUNCTIONS

The brief surge of adrenalin that bore her up during the encounter with Jarek and his henchmen soon deserted Seleva. She stepped along with determination, but every lift of a foot, every forward swing of her body, took more effort. She knew she should pause and call for help, but the stubborn pride that had carried her through her harsh life was still a factor in her character. She gritted her teeth and kept on.

At last she fell into darkness, protesting every inch and yet unable to keep herself from that welcome unconsciousness. When she came back to herself, she knew she was moving. Someone had made a litter of blankets, and she swung steadily from side to side, as the carriers matched their paces.

"Lemmon?" she asked, her voice sounding weak even to her own ears. "Falville? Yace?"

A hand caught her own, and she opened her eyes and looked up into Lemmon's anxious face. "Everything is fine. We're making good time, and Jon found his shortcut through the swamp along the stream, which saved us hours. You just rest. I have no idea what it is you are going to do, but it will take everything you have. You relax and let us do the work now. Your time will come."

Her other hand was caught by a small paw, and she turned her head to see Jon peering over the edge of the litter. "You are all right, Lady?" he asked, sounding fearful.

For a moment, the world spun again. How long had everyone within range depended upon her for comfort, guidance, and strength? Even now, when she could not stand on her feet, this child still clung to her for reassurance, and she could not bring herself to disappoint him.

"I am fine, Jon. You go ahead. Lead us quickly. I feel the time is passing fast, and we need to arrive as soon as possible. Things are moving toward each other...like stars...like ships...." She found to her horror that she had lost the thread of her meaning, and she went silent.

Closing her eyes, she tried to regain her orientation. She had to keep a clear head, to hold her purpose tightly, for she was the only person capable of controlling her grandson when the time came. Not even Jeroboah could manage that, for the old fellow was too absent-minded to keep his concentration focused on his work.

She must have slept for a time, for when she woke again it was late. The sky was murky, though there was no rain, and they had moved out from beneath the forest. Fields lay about them, and she tried to see across them as she was carried forward. Surely it was dangerous to go so openly, with day still staining the sky!

"Falville!" Her voice was once more her own. Though rather sharp with anxiety.

"Don't worry, Madame Karmann. We are hidden behind a planting of old orchards, and the watch points seem to be manned by only a few. We have avoided everything that looked threatening, we have passed the composting place Durk told about, and Jon tells me we will be near enough for you to direct us into the Stronghold before too long. He knows only the way from the town that his people used to visit. From here, he cannot help."

She knew there was something she should tell him, but her recalcitrant mind resisted her. Something important...but it would have to wait until later. She sighed and rested again. Now she found she began to recognize the countryside. That was the track leading to her own home farm, where Theron had thought he had her imprisoned. They had passed, long since, the winding way leading over the fields and through the copses to Jeroboah's concealed headquarters. After a time, she felt stronger, and her purpose again took control of her. They were very near....

Ahead! She made a motion with her hand, and Yace and Lemmon stopped and moved the litter so she could get to her feet. She swayed, for a moment, dizzy with weariness and the unusual motion. Then she steadied and looked about. It was dark, but the thin clouds diffused the starlight, and for eyes used to the dimness it was possible to see.

"At the end of that wall..."—she pointed to the stone barrier angled across their way—"...there should be a drain. We are too exposed here, for that is one of the outer defenses of the Stronghold. Come. We must hurry!" She went firmly toward the spot where the wall turned a corner, and the others came after her, their footsteps almost inaudible behind her.

She moved close up against the cold stone, running her right hand along it as she went, feeling for the symbol she had cut herself back in the days when quick escapes and secret returns were necessary to her survival. She halted as her fingers found the three-lobed mark she had made with a stonecutter's hammer back when she was forty years old and strong, and thought she knew all there was to know. She almost laughed as she started off again, bending now. She had remembered the trap she had set there as well.

"Here." She could hardly hear her own word, but the others had evidently been listening intently, for they came to a halt about her, as she reached and found a pair of strong hands. "Yace, you lift here. Falville, you bear down on the other side there. Yes. Lemmon, find a rock and wait to chock the slab, when it pivots upward. Jon, you get another for the other side. I must slip my hand between, once it rises, and disengage the trigger of my trap. Now. Heave!"

There was a grating sound as the slab, as large as a bed quilt and seemingly immovable, tilted slightly. Seleva reached and felt at one side, moving aside a flange of metal that kept the stone from betraying its mobility to anyone stepping on it. Beneath that was another, thinner strip, which she slipped cautiously back into its slot. "Now. Heave again!"

She could hear Yace grunt as he put his back into his effort. Falville shoved downward, and the stone pivoted on a central axis. Lemmon and Jon thrust big stones into the open sides, holding the thing wide enough to admit a man. A rush of damp, wretched-smelling air came puffing into her face, and Seleva leaned against the wall for a moment, her head spinning.

"Nasty," Lemmon gasped. "How long since this has been opened?"

"About forty years. Nobody knows about it but me. I had it put in as part of the drainage system, when I rebuilt the Stronghold, and nobody ever wondered why this branch of it was above the level of the sewage. It saved my life more than once. There are people who went to their graves wondering how I managed to disappear so completely and so quickly, when plots were hatched around me."

She stepped forward and lay flat to wriggle under the slab. She almost retched as the full impact of the stench washed over her, but she persisted, and soon she stood on the curve of dampish cement that formed the huge culvert. The others came through, coughing and gasping, and soon all were together in the darkness.

She drew their heads together closely, so her whispers would carry no farther than their circle. "There are grates, at intervals, that drain the paving of the walks and yards and the latrines of the barracks, as well as the slop waters from the kitchens. We do not know who might be up there, so we must not talk, and we must not show a light. Take hold of my coat, Lemmon. You, Falville, catch hers.

"Yace, you hold onto Lemmon with one hand and Jon with the other. Now, step softly, don't cough, and follow me." She staggered forward into darkness, pushing her balky body with every bit of will she possessed. Even after so many decades, her feet seemed to recognize the contours of the culvert, the curves of the way. She located herself by the falling of water from the first drain, which opened off to their right.

That was the kitchen yard drain. Yes. She turned into the first sharp-angled tunnel that branched slightly upward, and her companions' boots now scraped on a dry surface. She slowed, counting paces. They were beneath the barracks now, far enough from the real sewers for the stench to have lessened. Forty more steps took her to a cross tunnel, and she turned right, left into an intersecting way, then right again.

She reached to feel the wall, which was invisible in the pitch blackness. There was the first mark. Her fingers trailed along the wall, feeling the gritty plaster, still fresh-seeming after all its years of waiting for its sole user. She went on and on, following her old guides, until she came to the area for which she had headed.

The next marker ran beneath her hand, and the third. And then she felt the ring, set firmly into the concrete of the wall. "Now we can talk," she said. "We are beneath the solid cement of the Commander's quarters, and nothing less than a major explosion could make itself heard from here. I built that to be secure, and Theron has added his own unique designs.

"There is a set of rings, Falville. You are tallest, so I will ask you to reach up and find the next. Tie on the rope from your pack, for I am not the woman I was forty-odd years ago. I will need the help."

"Is it safe to strike a light?" asked Lemmon.

"Now it is. Yes."

There came a scritching of metal on metal, and one of the hand lamps blazed forth, its light seeming harshly brilliant after their long time in darkness. The rings shone dark—almost oily-looking—against the gray of the wall. Falville reached high to hook a loop of his rope into the second of them. Then he turned to look at Seleva. "Can you make it?" he asked.

"I will make it. You go up first. There is a metal cover above this set of rings. It can be moved clockwise, if you hook your fingers into the holes and push. It may require some strength, which is why I don't volunteer to go first. Above that is a service corridor leading from the kitchens to Theron's quarters. It should be empty at this time of night."

Without replying, Falville pulled himself up from ring to ring, setting his foot in the next-to-last as he reached up to move the cover. In a moment, he disappeared over the lip of the hole. In another moment Lemmon had tossed up the rope so he could help to lift Seleva's inconsiderable weight without requiring her to make the effort of climbing. She would have protested, but she knew she would need every bit of strength she possessed, once she gained her grandson's chambers.

Strangely, it was as she rode upward that her earlier thought recurred. "Falville," she called softly. "There is a computer imprint of my persona stored in the vault at my home, the Vineyards. Jeroboah will tell you where, if he can remember. But if not, call up the combination with my code: 'Theron'." She almost laughed as she went up and over the edge of the floor above her. "You may need something of my experience to draw upon before you are done."

She emerged into the corridor to see a dim light slanting across its farther end. Someone was awake there. "Check the kitchens," she whispered to Jon.

The boy darted silently down the hallway and disappeared around the corner. When he returned, he came close before breathing into her ear, "There's an old lady there. She looks a hundred. She's sitting at a table, and I think she's asleep."

"We must take care of this before we go forward," she said to Lemmon. "We can't have anyone giving the alarm until we have done what we came to do. Come with me.

"Falville, you and Jon stay here. Yace and Lemmon can control an old woman, if necessary, and I will see if I can get any sense from her of what is going on here in the Stronghold. Information never comes amiss."

Followed by the pair, Seleva crept down the hall and turned the corner, to see a woman who was most certainly not a hundred, whatever else she might be, sitting at a table and staring straight at the door as if expecting company. "Madame Karmann?" she asked, her voice steady and unafraid. "I have been waiting for you to come. Jeroboah told me you would."

Seleva breathed a thankful sigh and sank into a chair beside her. "Then for heaven's sake, get me a cup of tea. At my age, all this dashing around the countryside begins to get tiresome." She did not say that her bones had turned to water, and her heart was fluttering erratically in her bony chest. The information would help no one, and she knew she could force herself to last as long as need be.

The woman rose, and suddenly it was plain that she was not even past middle age, still strong and lithe. The gray wig she had worn slid from her hair, and she dropped it into a chair. When she returned with a steaming cup and a platter of cakes, Seleva watched as she wiped gray dust from her face. A remarkable resemblance emerged, and she smiled.

"So. This is what happened to Arvid's beautiful mother, who fled my grandson's advances. A wise move. It is good to have another set of hands to do the work before us."

"Not to mention a device that will remove the tenants of the control room, when that becomes necessary," said Lilias. She gestured toward an innocent-seeming barrel that stood in the corner beside the door. "I was not looking forward with any enthusiasm to moving it alone, but this young man can be of great help. It needs to go now, so I can reset the firing mechanism. Are you ready to begin?"

Seleva drained her cup, swallowed the last of her cake, and stood. "Indeed, we are ready to begin. Place that where you want it, and then we will go to visit the Commander of Station. It is time I face my grandson once again."

CHAPTER TWENTY-SIX

PERMUTATIONS

Standish had never felt so ill at ease before. Even the clean and mathematical music of Mozart could not soothe his unrest. He was cut off from the bulk of his troops now outside of Station; that was the thing that rankled. He touched a button, and the music died away. Bending over his table, he studied the contours of the countryside, the disposition of all known troops, and the blips of light and color that moved as new information came into the control room.

Karmann was on duty there, of course, and the thought still gave him some comfort. His cousin would never betray him. And Cozarre, should something unforeseen happen, could be trusted to push that scarlet lever into its slot. The assassin would not object to dying with the rest of Stronghold, even if he had known what would result from his action. Death was his mistress and his goal; it always had been, and the subsonic generators that were installed throughout the place would not distinguish between friend and foe.

His empty tray rattled as he sank into the deep chair beside the table on which it always sat. The old woman had not returned to get it—probably dozing in the mindless way of the aged. He would definitely have to dispose of her. She troubled him, no matter how well she cooked the things he most liked. He touched the button that rang in the kitchen. Then he sank back and closed his eyes. Things had gone so well! He was so nearly at the point at which Granary must inevitably fall into his hands, from the Wheatfields and Sterne Rift to the citrus groves of the southern peninsula, just north of the desert.

How had it come about that suddenly his great plans seemed to be crumbling in his hands? He had made no error of judgment. He had been as harsh and ruthless as possible. He could only believe that in some way his grandmother must be at the root of it, incredible as that might seem.

There came that damnably timid tap at the door. He checked the monitor, but only the gray, stooped figure of the kitchen woman stood there, head down as usual. He touched the unlocking button on the arm of his chair, and the door swung open. He heard footsteps in the corridor. Too many! Too heavy!

Whirling in his chair from the monitor to face the door, he stared up into the eyes of his grandmother. His heart chilled in his chest, and he felt his head begin to pound. This had to be a dream! Another nightmare, like those he had known in which Jeroboah came into his haven and taunted him face-to-face! He closed his eyes again and squeezed his forehead with one hand. This would go away, as those dreams of Jeroboah had, leaving him shaken but intact. But when he looked again, there stood Seleva, regarding him with cold silver eyes.

Behind her was the old woman, but now the gray coloration, the stooped walk, the tangle of hair half concealing her face were gone. It was Lilias Strindberg! That was why that resemblance had haunted him so!

He groaned and heaved to his feet. A man stepped forward and pushed him back, firmly but without violence. Another man, much younger, was on his other side, and a child now stared up at him from beside his strategy table. How had a child come here, into his most guarded center? How had even his grandmother made her way through his defenses?

"How did you come here? Who are these people?" His voice sounded hysterical, even to his own ears, and he breathed deeply, calming himself.

Before she could reply, there came another tap at the door. This one was neither soft nor timid, and when the woman who had been standing behind Lilias opened it, Jeroboah stood there, grinning. This was no dream, however he might long for it to be one. Standish lunged for the button that would alert the control room. Cozarre must push down the lever now!

* * * * * * *

Durk had followed Arvid, Jeroboah, and the others unquestioningly. He had done his bit, and now it was up to those who understood what was at stake to do theirs. But he watched as he went, his lazy wits finally waked to their native sharpness, and he could have led the party back along the intricate way they came, if it had been left to him to do. First they had gone underground for some time, following the course of a dry, subsurface stream. When they emerged, it was into a house in Station, and from it they went along an alleyway until they found a grate let into the paving to carry away rain water.

He noted that Jeroboah kept a small metal object in his hand all the way, and from time to time he would press a button on its face. Always they waited, at such times, until the old man nodded them onward. Durk suspected the thing in some way deactivated the traps Standish had in place about his Stronghold.

The storm sewer ran level below the walks above, and in time they found themselves beneath a grate that let them up into a curving corridor, which was empty. "You go along there," whispered Jeroboah to Durk. He pointed to the left. "There will be a brown door. Rap once on it, and when an answer comes, ask if the Questioner is ready. When she says she is, tell her to go to the control room. Then get out of sight at once. She should go immediately, and you will need to check if she has anyone in that chamber of horrors of hers. I am not willing for anyone to suffer her attentions."

He extended a withered hand, in which there was a lump of doughy stuff. "Know how to use this?" He took from another pocket of his colorless garment a packet containing the detonating devices and handed them over.

Durk nodded. He had been trained to use neoplastique in the military, and while he hated the stuff, he thought he could handle it.

"It will open that door for you." Jeroboah chuckled. "Now scoot."

Durk nodded and moved away, feeling he had been sent to do something childishly easy, because the older men had no confidence in his abilities. He looked along what seemed to be hundreds of white doors before finding the brown one, which was heavy duty metal extending from slots in the wall.

He rapped, just once, sharply with the hilt of his knife. After a few seconds, the speaker rasped, "Yes?"

"Is the Questioner ready?" he asked, though his voice wanted to shake.

"She is."

"Go to the control room at once," he said and began to back away.

But the door shot aside instantly, and a tall figure, all angles and hard fists and elbows, came bursting out upon him. Before he knew what had happened, Durk was rolling on the floor of the corridor, his teeth full of wiry black hair, his arms straining to hold a pair of claw-like hands away from his throat. It was a woman, he knew, though from the feel of her she was made of nothing but hard bones and leather. Her steely legs were clamped about his, her hands were moving irresistibly for his neck, and he had a sudden feeling that he was going to die.

His illness after escaping from the ward had left him weaker than he had ever been, and this bony harridan was going to throttle him and leave him lying on the hard floor while she charged off after his comrades. The thought filled him with furious energy, and he rolled desperately. She was strong, but she was lighter than he, and he managed to get on top of her and put his knees into her midriff. The hands kept grabbing painful parts of his anatomy, and he was hard put to keep his neck out of their grasp.

He suddenly bent sideways to distract her. Then he bounced forward and his forehead met her nose with a crunch of breaking cartilage. He felt as if he had run head-first into a boulder, but she was now lying still, her legs and arms flopping awkwardly on either side of her. For a moment, Durk lay flat on the rack of ribs and collarbone, catching his breath and wondering what sort of devil-woman this was. He found himself agreeing with Jeroboah: if there was anyone inside those doors who had been in her clutches, he was ready to get them out.

The brown door was still open, but he could see, past a small vestibule, solid metal interior doors, which seemed to be securely in place. He stumbled to his feet and moved to push on them, but they did not slip aside. The ball of explosive was still in the pocket into which he had put it. He took it out and molded it along the seam between the door panels.

The needle of the detonator went into place, and he backed away into the corridor before touching the tiny ignition device that had been in the packet Jeroboah gave him. There was a sputtering boom, and the door halves bowed apart, leaving a gap wide enough to see through.

The light in the room beyond was brilliant, and in its fierce illumination he saw a pale body hanging just above the floor. His vision still blurry from his throttling, he staggered forward and caught the limp shape, raising it from the punishing pressure on the shoulders. Holding her (he was sure this, too, was a woman) on one shoulder, he hacked away, the rope from the shackles binding her arms behind her. She came forward onto her face in his arms, and he turned her, laying her out flat on the bloodstained floor.

Then he turned and vomited all over his shoes. For this was

Sari, naked, her pale skin bearing the marks of a whip, her shoulders wrenched out of joint by the device on which she had hung. She looked dead. He turned back to her and knelt, putting his ear onto her chest. The skin was warm. There was still a heartbeat.

He found a ring of keys and unlocked the shackles, easing her over carefully to free her hands. He looked about for something to cover her, for she was beginning to shake, and he found a wide cloak of purple stuff that looked like something the dead woman outside might have worn when she rode her broomstick. There was a flask of pale liquid on the surgical table, but he didn't trust that. On a desk beyond it was a crystal decanter filled with what looked like wine. He tasted it cautiously, and it seemed all right. Then he lifted the girl's head and poured a drop between her pale lips.

Sari coughed. Her hands rose to her throat, and she opened her eyes.

Durk urged another sip on her. Her teeth chattered on the edge of the glass, and he held her around the shoulders, trying to lend her some of his own warmth. "It's all right now," he said, although he had no assurance of that at all. They might all be killed within the next few minutes. But she needed reassurance. "You saved me, Sari. I have never stopped thinking about you, and I'll take care of you for the rest of your life, if you'll let me." He tried to see if there was comprehension in her eyes.

The corner of her mouth lifted in the most fleeting of smiles. Then she was unconscious again, and he lifted her and carried her out into the corridor. As he stepped over the body of the Questioner, he heard a distant sound, like a shrill bell. And then there came an explosion that shook the entire length of the hallway in which he stood. He dropped to his knees and cushioned his burden by setting her in his lap. He would do well not to move until he knew what was going on, for he had no intention of risking Sari's life, just to satisfy his curiosity.

CHAPTER TWENTY-SEVEN

A GIFT IS DELIVERED

Garet hated it when Arvid assigned him solo tasks. And this one looked too simple, even though Jeroboah assured him that it was necessary. "If Theron has Cozarre in the control room, it means he has something particularly nasty for him to do. Cozarre is beyond that doorway. The barrel beside the door is going to explode before long, so you take shelter behind a solid corner, some distance down the hall.

"But once the thing goes off, and the opening of the door will do that, you must run as fast as you can, leaping dead bodies if necessary, to kill the man who will remain inside that room. This is so important I cannot find words strong enough for it. Believe me, I know Theron Standish, and I knew Cozarre. Between them, they will have something in reserve that will do for us, if we don't prevent it."

Jeroboah looked so stern and fierce, all his vagueness lost in his concern, that Garet almost believed the job was as vital as he claimed. So now he crouched behind a corner, waiting for an explosion. There was a dull thump, and he almost dived for the door before he realized it came from a considerable distance in the wrong direction. He settled back, waiting for his own signal.

He had moved to ease cramped muscles when there came a shrill ringing through the corridor. He huddled against the wall, waiting. The door grated into its slot, and feet pounded...another explosion, this one ear-splittingly near, made him hug the wall even more tightly. Missiles zipped along the hall that angled into the one in which he hid. Splats and chatters of impact sounded, along with more muffled thuds.

Garet rose and hurled himself up the hall, along the corridor and into the room. Those steel doors were smashed, their curved surfaces pocked with embedded bolts and nails, broken glass and small rocks. But he had no time to observe such things. He was diving for the burly man whose hand was already on a red switch. His own hands caught the other by the wrist and hurled both their bodies backward from the board holding the switch.

Cozarre was big and he was fast, but Garet was triggered to kill. He cut the man's throat before he could get his wits together. Well, by beef and barley, the old man had meant what he said. Garet had no idea what that switch would do, but the notices all around it said DO NOT TOUCH! AUTHORIZED PERSONNEL ONLY! and DANGER! That was enough for him. He was just as glad he didn't understand what fate he had just averted.

When he looked down at his boots, he realized he must have run through blood as he entered the place. A glance outside told him that what remained of the other men (he couldn't even tell how many there might have been) was past any help or hurt. He was happy he had missed that fate as well. They had evidently been blasted as they ran from the control room.

* * * * * * *

Three heartbeats thudded into the past, and a muffled explosion shook even Standish's deep and reinforced chambers. What could that be? Destructive sonic devices were almost silent, only shaking masonry and flesh into their component molecules. He stared wildly at Seleva, but she shook her head.

"This is no work of mine. You can credit Lilias and Jeroboah, if you like. But your cousin Karmann and your other officers are no longer, I suspect, among the living. Your signal to the guardroom has sprung a trap. When we have done with you, there will be no ambitious young officers with delusions of grandeur left to try rekindling your Grand Scheme from its ashes. You have not created an empire, Theron.

"When Karmann (I know it was he, for he has always come running when you called) opened that door, it set off the greeting Lilias concocted from things so unsophisticated that you would never have called them the stuff of weaponry." Dazed as he was, he saw pain in her eyes, and suddenly he remembered that Karmann, too, was her kin.

The youngster they called Yace caught her gaze, nodded, and left the room. Theron could hear his steps running along the corridor—going to check on the effect of their trap, he was certain.

"Then kill me now. I expect nothing else." Suddenly the thought of death was comforting. Once dead, he could not be called to account for the things he had done or caused to be done. His head was buzzing with visions and memories with things he realized that he hated to recall. With sudden clarity, he remembered that dream of being in the hospital, of being carted away to that hellish pit where the bodies of his enemies made compost to enrich his crops. Would they put his body there, to furnish fertilizer for the crops of Station? He shivered.

Seleva smiled, and it was not a comforting thing to see. "We have no intention of killing you. We are going to cure your madness."

Standish half rose from his chair, but the burly man who was Lilias's son pushed him back again. Suddenly every nerve was screaming with fear. Was this what those he sent into battle or, worse yet, to the Questioner, felt as they went? He needed to vomit, and his bowels opened, soiling his trousers and the chair.

"Hold him, Arvid," said his grandmother. She looked into his eyes, and he realized he saw pity there. No anger. No fear. No revulsion. Only pity.

"Theron," she said, her words slow and distinct. "Listen to me. I have traveled a great distance and suffered as you will never live long enough to suffer, in order to save your life and your mind. If this does not work, you will be killed. If you do not respond to this shock I am about to give you and accept this hard-won gift I bring, you will die, and all your talents and skills will be lost to our people. They need you, Theron Standish, Commander and thinker. They do not need a man sunk deeply into paranoia. Do you understand?"

He struggled as his body was wrapped round and round with strips torn from the tablecloth. He felt his eyes going wide, like those of a frightened horse, and her words almost failed to penetrate his frantic mind.

She slapped him, hard. He blinked, bringing himself under control.

"Listen to me, Standish. We are valuable, you and I, to our world. I am old, but I have preserved most of my memories, skills, and abilities by means of my computer system. You are still relatively young. Between us, we can benefit our world. With the skills you have and the contacts you have made, added to the things you can learn from my computerized persona, you can help Granary to hold its autonomy and continue to command favorable terms of the Traders. You can preserve, instead of destroying, the freedom of this colony.

"To do that you must live! Dead, you are only a resource in a computer. Alive you are a functioning mind, with unique capacities for problem-solving. But you are mad. As you sit here, tied and helpless, you are mad. Do you understand me?"

He did not, of course, but he gasped a smothered, "Yes."

"Then it is time. This is the pain you have caused to be inflicted on others. This is the agony of those caught in the blasts of flame-throwers and lasers. Feel their deaths, Theron. Feel their deaths."

She took from her belt a small silver box. Jeroboah, beside her, took her hand and held it for an instant, staring down at the thing she grasped, a tragic expression on his withered face. She looked up at him, over at her grandson, down at the child. She reached blindly for the scarred man beside her, and he pulled her close in a hug.

The small, tough-looking woman touched her shoulder, and Theron could see tears in eyes that he intuitively knew had seldom wept. Something inside him, long sealed and inaccessible, seemed to crack along unsuspected lines. No one had ever touched him so, had ever wept for him, except, long ago, this strange old woman who was his grandmother.

He closed his eyes as she pulled free of those about her and moved toward him. The silver box was in her hand, held out toward his bare arm. He felt her hand on his skin, the coolness of the metal box. A tingling...what was that? It felt as if tiny roots were moving down through his pores, into his nerve-endings. There was a rustling of her clothing, a creaking of her old joints. She had gone to her knees beside him. Her arm lay along his, only the sharp angles of the box between the layers of their skin.

What was this? What was she trying to do? No torture he had ever learned had begun in such a manner. Then the torture began, and he realized that his experience of pain had touched only its sur-face. Now he learned what it was to feel the lick of flame, the plas-tered jelly burning into his own body-fat, his bones melting.

He felt his life go out in a sear of agony, and then there was grateful blackness...only to be succeeded by a fall from some high place, turning over and over as his breath left his lungs and his heart cramped with panic. The end, his bones crunching and shattering, his life snatched away in a gasp of anguish, was not the end of his journey.

He was burned and crushed, riddled with pellets, skewered with arrows, punctured with the beams of lasers, and drowned in his own blood. Death after death sucked him under dark waves, and time af-ter time he was unwillingly resurrected, only to die again.

"This is not illusion," his grandmother's voice said, softly and yet so clearly the words sank through his brain and into his very bones. "This is reality. These people suffered and they died, all because you must control an entire world. I learned, Theron, late in life and yet, I hope, not too late, that no single person has the judgment or the ability or the self-control to manage an entire world and its people, according to his own whim. Our population is small as yet, but it will grow if Granary is managed well.

"Even a wonderfully wise and just person is not qualified for such power. You were certainly not that, nor was I. I did what I must, and then I stepped down, hoping you would do better. I was criminally wrong, and now I must pay for it. More, perhaps, than you." Her voice was growing thin.

He knew with sudden clarity that she was feeling everything he endured. She had used her own body to amplify the content of that hellish box, and the anguish was slowly killing her. He could feel her life waning, even as he suffered and died again and again.

Someone was screaming, great tearing shrieks of agony that rang through his rooms. Then he realized his throat was raw. It was his own voice that disturbed the walls that were used only to the strains of music of the ancient masters. He opened his eyes and stared down at the slight arm holding that terrible box against him.

"Please!" he gasped. "Oh, please!" A feeling of despair, of violation, and of helpless rage filled him, and he did not know if it came from his own responses or were sensations trapped in that damnable box.

She shook her head, though now she had wilted against his chair, and Lemmon and Lilias were holding her up so that she could continue her work. "No. You are still the Theron you have been. I see it in your eyes. Not until a different Theron looks out at me will I stop. Not until I die will I give up this thing that I have worked so hard to bring about."

Then the scarlet tide washed over him again. He thought he fainted, from time to time, but always there was water at his lips, bringing him back to face that unswerving will that had brought to him the suffering of his people. His people...his mind, retreating as far as possible from the convulsions of his body, thought about that. They had seemed to be cattle, convenient for his purposes. But had they been more? Did they have the same feelings he did? She was proving to him that their nerves reacted just as his did to unbearable stresses.

Those boys he had misused, when he tired of torturing girls, what had they felt? What had become of the ones who lived? He had known them only as toys made of flesh, but now he understood what suffering flesh was capable of undergoing, and he knew an emotional pain that matched the one his grandmother imposed on his nerves.

The farmers, whom he had regarded with contempt because they worked and sweated and walked in manure and mud...were they men like himself, with needs and ambitions, dreams and hopes? He had never before considered the possibility. The soldiers he sent to kill those resisting him were living bodies tenanted by unique spirits. Why had he never suspected that? Each final agony, every death proved it to him more and more emphatically. For every death, he learned, was different.

Time became a river with neither beginning nor end. His heart, convinced that he was dying, had to be stimulated by some device Jeroboah carried with him, or it would have failed completely. His grandmother, when he could bring himself to look at her, seemed transparent, growing as wispy as fog, while she suffered the things she transferred into him.

When the process stopped at last, he didn't understand it for a time. His nerves still shrieked with jolts of agony, and his mind was whirling with concepts that had never troubled his thoughts before. When the strips were unbound, his arm freed of that awful silver box, he hardly knew who he was or what had occurred. Something was held to his lips, and he sipped hot, spicy liquid that cleared his head miraculously.

Lilias was holding it. He looked into her eyes and understood, at last, what it was he had done to her and to her family. He had tried to deal with her as if she were a machine or a doll, ignoring her rights and emotions as a human being. She had done what he would have done, if their positions had been reversed, and he had hounded her and her children because of it.

He leaned to vomit onto his precious carpet, emptying his belly and purging himself of much that he had been. When he was able to see again, he felt the tension in the room. There was something wrong. He felt it in the woman, that other one they called Lemmon, the men, and the child. Their faces were grim, their lips set, and tears stood in their eyes, as they lifted his grandmother from her place beside his chair.

And then he knew. The arm that had lain upon his for so long hung limp. Her eyes were open, their silver now shallow and without life. Her delicate face, so youthful even at her advanced age, had sunk into deep-cut lines. She was, without any doubt, dead at last. He could smell her death hanging in the air about him.

He looked up at the scarred and soldierly man who was examining the strategy table. "Why?" he asked, almost too exhausted to speak the word. "Why?"

* * * * * * *

Falville stared down at the Commander of Station. Another man looked, now, from those bloodshot eyes. The voice was not the demanding and arrogant one everyone knew. This was a broken man... broken to their purposes. The thought did not make Falville feel anything but ill.

"Your grandmother wanted to change you without killing you. Your skills are desperately needed, but your ambitions and your lusts are impossible to allow to continue. Without your contacts with the Traders off-world, we would have to relearn from the beginning the strategies by means of which we can hold our own. Otherwise, we might make serious errors, abrogating the treaties your grandmother stained her soul to gain. What is written in books or stored in computer files cannot match what exists in a living mind, which can adapt and adapt again, at need.

"She suffered because of the things she did as a leader. She was determined that if you could be salvaged, your training, your intelligence, and your abilities would be of great advantage to our world. She could not bear the thought that we should sink again into the dependency and near slavery other agricultural worlds endure. Can you understand that?"

The silver eyes, so like Seleva's, closed briefly. When they opened again, the man nodded. "Yes," he gasped.

Falville nodded, feeling at last that all the effort, the pain, and the death had been worth it. "Jeroboah, old as he is, addled as he seems most of the time, knew this was the right thing. Drifting between the past and the present, he still managed to do the necessary things, when the time came, to allow us to succeed. As well, I suspect, as paying you visits, by means of a holographic image.

"For he tells me that he has had a way to control all of your electronic equipment since the beginning. He designed the system, as you would know if you had studied the records of your grandmother's reign. If there had been an organization within Station capable of restraining you, he could have let its leaders into your sanctuary at any time. But things had to work themselves out. Competent and dedicated people had to be in place, and the device he invented for Seleva to steal was the one thing that would make the difference for our people."

Falville sighed and turned toward the door, almost feeling pity for this erring, broken man. "I must go and help Arvid Strindberg, who is now in charge of the Stronghold. Rest, Commander of Station. Your work—your real work—has only just begun, here on Granary."

CHAPTER TWENTY-EIGHT

ENDINGS AND BEGINNINGS

Although it would be many weeks yet before General Coville could bring his people down from the snowbound heights, Falville realized very soon that it was not a problem. Strindberg's people moved swiftly to make contact with the rebels in Ellanish. When they met Standish's troops, they were armed with orders from the Commander himself, validated with his personal imprint, as well as ratified by orders sent along the command channel.

For himself, he felt weary and empty. He had not realized, in the brief time he had known her, how much impact Seleva Karmann had made upon him. Lemmon, too, seemed deflated, though she went about her work of organizing the new occupation of Stronghold in her normal efficient way. Yace and Jon, however, seemed inconsolable.

Now there was no graver matter to attend, Falville went about trying to find work for them that would cheer them by keeping them busy. It was in doing so that he found the hospital run by Nurse Sari. To call it a hospital was, he thought, obscene. The rough shack at the edge of the area inside the walls of Stronghold still held half a dozen badly injured troopers—two women, four men. Gottenrod had taken flight, it was evident, when the Commander changed, for he had not been seen in some time.

Sari, from her bed in the regular hospital, managed to draft, with Durk's help, a number of strong backs and willing spirits to help with dredging out the place and removing the remaining patients to treatment and comfort. The two worked together, he noted with amusement, as if they had known each other for years. He suspected their partnership would become permanent. Mutual suffering was, perhaps, a powerful bond. Almost as powerful as the feeling they tried to keep from showing when others were around.

Yace had turned to helping them with vigor, and Falville knew he was impressed with the young woman who drove him so hard. He seemed to assume that she would be, in time, something of a sister-in-law to him. Jon lent his fleet legs to any errand-running, and the two seemed fairly content, as they helped to make order of the chaos that was Station, after the destruction of the officer-staff of Standish's organization.

Dropping by to check on progress in demolishing the old Disciplinary Ward, Falville joined his steps with those of a young man who was going in that direction. He was staring about, as if reacquainting himself with the place, and Falville was interested.

"Have you been here before?" he asked.

To his surprise, the boy's eyes filled with tears. "I spent days here before I escaped. I've been putting off going back. I'm afraid... I'm afraid Sari may have been caught and killed, before things changed. I can't decide whether it's better to know or not to know."

Falville put out a hand and patted the boy's shoulder. "She's alive," he told him. "I have been visiting her regularly. They caught her, Gottenrod and his henchmen, and took her to the Questioner, but she is alive, and she will heal. They assure me of that. Come and see her."

As they went toward the hospital, he wondered how many others owed their lives to the nurse's courage. He felt satisfaction when he thought of her as mistress of Durk's waiting farm and home...she deserved it all and more. He only wished....

And even as he wished, they met Lemmon hurrying along on some errand for Coville, who was organizing the city with typical efficiency. She smiled at him, as she always had, as if there were no terrible scar ruining half his face. Perhaps he, too, might find solace and affection, when all was finished and he was able to return to his own work again.

* * * * * * *

Yace had been happy to find Durk among those who had followed Strindberg into station. "Durk, we'll go back to Ellanish together, when things are whipped into shape here," he told his old friend. "We can run your farm together, if you'll let me help. My folks were killed early, and they never owned land anyway. And Jon will be a lot of help, too."

He reached to tousle the hair of the child. "Maybe we can get some of the others who haven't anything to go back to. They could come too, and we'd be able to do wonders. What do you think?"

Things were coming too fast. Durk found himself hard put to keep up with Yace's words, "The farm? It's still mine? And the house?" He frowned. "My father's gone. How could we know what was best to do? He always planned everything."

"Don't worry about that," said the little boy. "Yace knows everything!"

Yace chuckled. "He'll outgrow that, but while it lasts, it's nice. We can get advice from the others. Things should be getting organized pretty well back home by now. We left a lot of angry people putting things together again as fast as they could. When the ground thaws, crops are going into the soil more quickly and with better planning than they ever have before. We're ready to farm again. Soldiering is for people who like to kill. And to die." His exuberant tone had become thoughtful.

"Falville!" he called after the tall soldier. "We all want to go home together, when the time comes. Think it's all right?"

The man turned and smiled at them. "We will all be going home soon. But wait to see what is needed before you go. I suspect we still have work to do before we leave Station. When the time comes, you will be told."

Yace sighed, but he knew the officer was right. He pitied the people of Station, who were only gradually coming to realize they no longer had to creep about silently, dreading the whims of their mad Commander.

* * * * * * *

Jeroboah sat in Standish's chair, staring at the monitors above the table. The Commander of Station had gone to his grandmother's house for a long rest. Lemmon accompanied him, as much to nurse his battered mind and body as to make certain that his reformation was more than skin deep. Lemmon would also have time to recover from the loss of Seleva, for the young woman had grown very close to the older one.

Jeroboah thought Falville, who accompanied the group going to the Vineyards, might well have a hand in cheering the troopmistress. He had caught the officer's expression when he looked at her, and he knew people. Falville's scarring would heal somewhat, and there would be surgeons, once trade was normalized, who could do much to correct the damage. But even if that didn't happen, he felt Lemmon didn't really see the surface any longer, after working so hard and through such danger with the man behind that face.

Strindberg had returned to the forest, taking with him Nedra, his mother, and his father. They had lived too long in the free ranges of the wood and the mountains to go back to the confinement of caring for crops and livestock. Now, however, they would not prey upon their neighbors, for their neighbors would no longer hunt them. Jeroboah thought good things would come from the forest people in time.

Seleva was gone. That left him by far the oldest human being on Granary, and he found it lonely. He needed another trip into the mountains, once spring thawed the snows. Perhaps he would find his own end there, in the clean air and the untroubled ways of the birds and beasts. That would be good. He was growing too absent-minded to be of much use any longer.

Coville and his people would see to Granary now, supervising Standish, even after he returned to duty, as he trained people to deal with the Consortium and the Traders. It would be a good combination.

The shuttle would rise again, bearing cargoes of grain and fruit, of dried meat and wine and vegetables, ready for trade with hungry spacers. And useful tools would come back down from the platform, making the work of the farmers easier and the lives of the people more comfortable.

He sighed. His work was done, and he longed to rest his gaze upon green forests and snowy peaks. Soon it would be spring. Granary was ready for that, and so was he. He rose and touched a button. The monitors blanked out. The strategy table went dark. And Jeroboah left the quarters of the Commander of Station for the very last time.

EPILOGUE

THERON STANDISH

Standish stood on the long veranda of his grandmother's house. The vines that overhung the arbors overhead were once more thick with leaves and new clusters of tiny grapes. He had survived the terrible winter, and now he felt as fragile and thin as if he had been dreadfully ill and only now had recovered.

He heard footsteps behind him, and he turned to meet the gaze of the young woman who had been put in charge when Lemmon returned to her post at Coville's side. Nurse Sari seemed able to ignore her treatment at the hands of his torturer, though she would never again move with the ease she had known in the past.

Theron felt himself go stiff, and he tried to relax and smile as she offered him a cup of hot herb tea. "There is something your grandmother wanted you to do," she said. "We found her instructions when we retrieved her personal file from her computer system, though she insisted that if you survived you must be well before you do this. Durk and I have decided you are now well enough."

He gave a snort, thinking of the brash young man who had come with Sari to oversee the farm until it was time for the couple to return to their own home in Ellanish. The boy hated him, that was certain, but the control he showed made Theron feel immature by comparison. He had never been able to say no to his own impulses with the iron will this youngster possessed.

He sipped the content of the cup, grimacing at the sharp flavor. But he knew if he refused it, Sari would insist on his drinking it with the gentle firmness of a child's governess. When he was done, he followed her into his grandmother's study and set the cup on a table.

He felt his chest tighten. Jeroboah sat before Seleva's console, his wrinkled fingers playing over the keys. He looked even tinier than before, and Standish had a feeling he would not see the old man again.

"Come in, Theron," he said. "Your grandmother left a message for you, and I am calling it up right now. She hoped all the way through that you would survive. And you did, thanks to her. Now you must listen to her once again, for the last time."

"I want no message from Seleva," Theron said. His voice seemed choked in his throat, and his eyes were blurred with tears. He could remember clearly his attempts to find and to kill her, while all the time she was painfully collecting her final gift for him.

He was now another person, although he had not quite decided who that was. He had already begun dealing with problems sent from the Stronghold, as the temporary Commander, General Coville, tried to re-establish the damaged links with the Traders. He found his mind worked as well as before, perhaps better.

However, he realized he had been seeing everyone through a cracked mirror before, suspecting treachery where there was none, fearing for his life in dealing with people who meant him no harm. The shock of pain and repeated death had shown him reality, and that made him understand that the things he had feared were tenuous and unreal. The stuff of dreams or nightmares.

Yet he still felt a certain tenderness. Guilt there was and would be, he suspected, for as long as he lived. Beyond that there was a hesitancy in dealing with others, for fear he might lapse into his bad old ways. And now that would mean instant, painless death. Sari had her orders, and if she faltered, Durk would not.

Jeroboah linked the computer with the holo and touched one last key. "I will go now," he said. "You sit here, where Seleva sat for so many years, and listen to her. And Theron, do your best to understand what it is she is telling you."

Then he was gone, and Theron Standish watched the holographic image of his grandmother form over the magnetic plate of the mechanism. Half life-size, she turned toward the chair in which he sat. To his surprise, she was smiling. That was an expression he had seldom seen her wear, for she had been dealing energetically with myriad problems and plots, even when he was a youngster. Now she looked...grandmotherly.

"So you have come through, Theron. I am happy you did. There are things you can do for Granary, carrying forward policies that will make us a world to which the Traders and the Cooperative of Worlds will listen, in time.

"You never liked to study history. That is a pity, for much of our trouble has come because of historic attitudes toward agricultural worlds on the part of the Consortium. Farmers are considered to be, in some way, less intelligent than factory workers or clerks or computer experts. This perception has come down through human history, having its roots, I suspect, on old Terra itself.

"So the agricultural worlds were set up almost as fiefdoms of governors set over them to pull from their soils the most possible produce for the least possible payment. That is a thing I set out to change, here on our own planet. And I succeeded. For this to continue, we must present a united front to everyone else.

"When the representatives of the Traders come to inspect our facilities, there must be no hint of the war we have just fought. Nobody must mention anything about attacks or tortures or paranoia.

"You are Commander of Station, as you have been since my retirement. You must persuade them their information is faulty, if they ask about recent problems here."

She moved as if her back were painful to her, and he thought of the kilometers she had walked, the mountains she had climbed, the misery she had endured on his behalf. But she was not done. "I learned almost too late that ruthlessness will only achieve a certain amount. After that, it is self-defeating. I killed and I kidnapped. I blustered and blarneyed and succeeded at first, because I was in a position of strength. Ours is one of the very few worlds producing food that will keep spacers healthy without supplementary diet, and this gave me the leverage I needed.

"But there came a time when I was faced with dissension among my own people. I continued my bad old ways, and I was not overthrown because there was nobody to take my place. A change of command at that time would have left us open to another takeover by the Traders and the Cooperative. I was the lesser of two evils, and the people did not rebel. Not openly."

Now the pale-skinned face turned grim. "It was the deaths of your parents that made me understand my own errors. I caused them, though not knowingly. I learned from them, although I had been intended to die with my daughter and her husband."

"You caused their deaths?" Standish had wondered all his mature life what had happened on that journey into Sterne Rift. His grandmother had returned alone, shutting herself away for a long while, letting her lieutenants do the work of Station. His parents had come back in ornate coffins, to be cremated at home.

She seemed to have known he would need a moment in which to think, for she paused. Now she continued, "A bomb was set in the carrier we used. I was called back to take a message from Station, and so I was not inside when the driver started the mechanism.

There was nothing left of anyone, only smears of blood and metal dust.

"The coffins at the cremation were empty. You were only twenty, so I said nothing to you. They were dead; why should you suffer even more?" Tears were shining on her cheeks, now, and her eyes seemed to be staring into some painful place she knew too well.

"At that point, I began to learn. It was a slow process, for your hard head was inherited directly from me. Your grandfather, if you had known him, would have surprised you. This Vineyard was his life-long work, and he was as gentle as I was harsh. I did not learn as easily and unresistingly as he would have done.

"Yet from that point forward until my retirement I thought twice before making drastic decisions affecting people's lives and deaths. I became less quick, but I also became more human. As the years passed, I knew that while my earlier actions had been, to some extent, justified by the conditions I faced, they would not work in a peaceful and productive society.

"Theron, they did not work for you. They produced the rebellion that brought down your dream of becoming the ultimate tyrant. While I was a part of that, I was only a small part. When many people reach the limits of their patience, things change. That has been true all through history, and I urge you to read in my library, while you complete your recovery. I commend to your notice the books about Terra.

"Only when military aggression against its own countries stopped and those who were planetary brothers began cooperating did our ancestors succeed in their ambitions for moving into other worlds. Over the millennia, over the warps, they have begun to forget that now, but we on Granary are here to remind them again.

"That may be your most important project. Send carefully written, closely reasoned messages to the Chancellors of the Cooperative, showing them, from the basis of our historical past, that some of the recent policies of their body are unwise. You may not succeed, Grandson, but you will at least have tried."

She turned those silver eyes upon him, and now she looked very serious. "Even when you were maddest, even when you wanted my death, I have loved you, Theron Standish. You are my blood and bone, my hope for the future. Now finish your healing. Go back and do the work waiting for your unique abilities. And take with you the blessing of Seleva Karmann."

The hologram died to mist, and Standish sat staring at the emptiness where his grandmother's shape had formed. He heard steps come to the door, wait for a time, and go away again. He said nothing.

For Theron Standish, reluctantly and at long last, was altering his ambitions for the future.

ABOUT THE AUTHOR

The author of seventy books, more than forty of them published commercially, **ARDATH MAYHAR** began her career in the early eighties with science fiction novels from Doubleday and TSR. Atheneum published several of her young adult and children's novels. Changing focus, she wrote westerns (as **Frank Cannon**) and mountain man novels (as **John Killdeer**), four prehistoric Indian books under her own name, and historical western *High Mountain Winter* under the byline **Frances Hurst**.

Recently she has been working with on-line publishers. *A Road of Stars* was her first original novel to appear in print-on-demand format. Many of her out-of-print titles are now available from e-publishers fictionwise.com and renebooks.com; many other novels are being published by the Borgo Press Imprint of Wildside Press and Amazon.com.

Now in her seventies, Mayhar was widowed in 1999, after forty-one years of marriage, and has four grown sons. She now works at home, writing short fiction and nonfiction, and doing book doctoring professionally. Her web pages can be found at:

w2.netdot.com/ardathm/

and

http://ofearna.us/books/mayhar.html

www.ingramcontent.com/pod-product-compliance
Lightning Source LLC
Chambersburg PA
CBHW050743250626
47155CB00005B/1903